“Tell me wl
murmured

“You know.” Tra
resisted the urge to cross her arms over her chest. Paul wanted her to lie here and request items off the menu? Name her own body parts? She swallowed. “Touch me.”

“Okay.” He kept up the stroking until his warm strong fingers brushed up under her breasts, then down to the waistband of her jeans. She arched, hungry for a more intimate touch.

He undid her jeans, slid his hand inside, almost there, still not enough, making her tremble and strain for him. “Here?”

“No.” She’d come apart too soon. He should be with her. “Not like that.”

“Yes. I want to see you let go.”

“No. I want you to…oh no.” She clutched at his arm, but he kept going until she gave in, cried out and exploded into her climax.

She went limp against him, still panting. “I thought I was doing this for you.”

“Believe me, you were,” he said. “That was the sexiest thing I’ve ever seen.”

Dear Reader,

THE MANHUNTERS miniseries chronicles the adventures of Tracy, Allegra, Cynthia and Missy, who set out to explore the phenomenon of instant attraction. Is it lust? Love? Or a completely humiliating trick of their hormones?

I met my husband for the first time at night. All I could see was a dark blob sitting on a porch. But when our friend introduced us, I got a weird electric shiver. I know it sounds nuts, and it's a tad embarrassing to admit to, but it's true. Of course at the time, I didn't pay much attention, since I'd never dated any dark blobs and wasn't sure I wanted to start.

However, the next day I met him in broad daylight and got an even bigger jolt. We were married two years later.

I hope you enjoy Tracy and Paul's story. Write to me with tales of your own instant attraction. Did it last? A second? An hour? A lifetime? I'd love to hear. You can send e-mail via my Web site at www.IsabelSharpe.com.

Cheers,

Isabel

P.S. Allegra, Missy and Cynthia's MANHUNTER stories follow in a double Duets next month!

Books by Isabel Sharpe

HARLEQUIN DUETS

17—THE WAY WE WEREN'T
26—BEAUTY AND THE BET
32—TRYST OF FATE
44—FOLLOW THAT BABY!

HARLEQUIN BLAZE

11—THE WILD SIDE

HOT ON HIS HEELS

Isabel Sharpe

TORONTO • NEW YORK • LONDON
AMSTERDAM • PARIS • SYDNEY • HAMBURG
STOCKHOLM • ATHENS • TOKYO • MILAN • MADRID
PRAGUE • WARSAW • BUDAPEST • AUCKLAND

This book is dedicated to Cherie, Sandee, Sharon and Vicki, who gently and firmly got me through it, sick kids, winter blahs and all.

ISBN 0-373-25973-5

HOT ON HIS HEELS

This edition published by arrangement with Harlequin Books S.A.

Visit us at www.eHarlequin.com

Printed in U.S.A.

1

TRACY RICHARDS took her customary flying leap off the third-to-last step of her parents' deck and landed on the soft sand...forgetting she was wearing pumps.

"*Ouch.*" Her ankle wobbled painfully. "Bleeping heels."

She strode furiously toward Lake Michigan to retrieve a towel left out earlier in the day. Or at least she tried to stride furiously. But striding furiously across sand in bleeping heels and...much worse...*panty hose* was ludicrous. In fact, even having to wear them was ludicrous. Who wanted to get dolled up at the beach? Especially when it was this muggy.

But her dad had an image of overwhelming success to uphold, or whatever he thought he was doing. The need to strut his opulence had gotten worse since Tracy's mom died a year ago. As if he were trying to honor her memory by indulging as much as possible in the luxury she'd craved all her life. Luxury she'd only been able to enjoy for a few short years before a heart attack took her away.

So now, when her dad threw parties here at their summer "palace" in Door County, Wisconsin—parties that were recently suspiciously stocked with wealthy unattached men Tracy's age—everyone dressed up.

She thought longingly of the July Fourth parties the family had growing up on their farm in Oak Ridge before the family business took off. Cheap beer in plastic cups, chips still in the bag and bratwurst tossed on the grill, guests in shorts and jeans and whatever they felt like.

Now it was gourmet-catered this and stemware holding vintage that. Enough to make you want to hurl rabbit cilantro sausage across the room. Thank goodness her three closest friends had come up to Fish Creek from Milwaukee for the weekend or she'd feel even more out of place in her own family's house than she already did.

She reached the forgotten towel and shook it savagely. Immediately, the humid breeze coming off the lake blew gritty grains of sand between her contacts and her eyeballs. She doubled over, eyes squeezed shut and streaming.

Bleeping sand. Bleeping breeze. Bleeping—

"You okay?"

She stifled a groan. Jake. Son of her dad's most recent set of close friends who happened to be gazillionaires. He'd been following her around all day like a dog promised extra kibbles with his bits.

"Sand in my contacts." She opened her eyes, blinked cautiously, and turned in relief. "Whew. It's—"

Electricity rushed into her body as if she'd suddenly become a power station.

Not Jake. Not at all Jake. Not even *remotely* Jake.

Tousled thick blond hair needing a cut. Strong masculine chin needing a shave. Tall muscular body wearing the kind of scruffy comfortable clothes she'd be wearing if she could. Breathing deeply as if he'd been jogging. And behind dime-store sunglasses lurked eyes that were giving her lessons in chemistry the likes of which she experienced only in her fantasies. God forbid he took his shades off. She'd probably climax right here on the beach.

His eyebrows quirked up over the top of his glasses and she realized it would probably be polite to put her tongue back into her mouth—figuratively speaking of course. "Sorry for staring. I...thought you were going to be someone else."

"As far as I know I've always been me." He gave a quick grin and moved past her. "Glad you weren't dying of anything. See you around."

She turned, clutching the towel to her chest with both fists, and watched him jog up the beach. Why did that happen sometimes? Some guys you could stare at all day and not get a single quiver, even if they were drop-dead gorgeous, and some guys...some guys could turn you inside out with a single glance. Even a single glance from behind dark lenses.

Tracy gave the towel another more careful shake, folded it, and started reluctantly back across the beach to the house, stomach heavy with a strange restless disappointment. If she had any guts she would have kicked off her heels and jogged after him down the beach, or better still, smiled a sultry smile and invited him to join the party, instead of turning into a tongue-tied hormonal mess. He was just the kind of guy she always fell for. Casual, a little scuffed around the edges, and not dripping a single dollar sign. Like the guys she grew up with in Northwest Wisconsin.

But then he hadn't exactly seemed to want to linger. Hadn't he felt the sizzling charge between them? Could she experience a connection that powerful all on her own? It didn't seem possible.

She climbed up the steps to her parents' deck and gave one last searching gaze up the beach for a certain fabulously put-together jogger in gray running shorts and a white T-shirt sporting the logo for Attitude! clothes. Regardless, he was gone. She'd missed her chance. Now it was back to the party, back to foie gras and fresh currants on toast points and fending off the Jakes of Door County. She shaded her eyes and stared harder. Was that him off in the distance? She couldn't tell. The shores of Lake Michigan weren't exactly empty in July, even in this exclusive part of the peninsula.

"Enjoying the view?"

Tracy swung around. Her Milwaukee friends, Cynthia, Missy and Allegra had ambled out onto the deck. Cynthia, elegant in a beige linen sheath and pearls, toasted Tracy with her martini. "We started without you. Any buns out there worth scoping?"

"Shh! Cynthia!" Missy's chin-length blond hair swung against her bright red cheeks as she turned to see if any other guests had come out onto the deck. "Someone might *hear* you."

"So what?" The tall sophisticated brunette shrugged her expensively padded shoulders. "It's a free country. I defend my right to scope buns."

"I brought you something to drink, Tracy." Allegra handed over a frosty bottle of some fancy beer Tracy's dad stocked now, and flung back her frizzy mass of dark hair—the current choice from her vast collection of wigs. "Man it's stifling out here. So, what *is* the latest bun report? Or were you admiring other natural wonders?"

"Well..." Tracy rubbed her thumb along a scratch on the cedar deck railing, on the one hand bursting with starry-eyed excitement and on the other strangely reluctant to talk about the encounter. It had been so powerful, and would sound sort of stupid put into words. Cynthia would make a lewd remark, Missy would be embarrassed and Allegra would take it all in stride in her carefree Bohemian manner.

"Aha!" Cynthia's eyes narrowed. "I detect a close encounter of the masculine kind. Give, Tracy."

Missy rolled her eyes. "If she doesn't want to talk about it, she doesn't have to."

"Of course she does. Tell."

The women stared expectantly, Cynthia with eyebrows raised, Missy with reluctant fascination and Allegra with cheerful curiosity.

Tracy smiled and shook her head. She might as well. They'd get it out of her one way or another.

"Okay, okay. I was on the beach, and this guy came by and..." She gestured helplessly. How did one describe a wonder of the universe? "Have you ever made eye contact with a total stranger and just about died from the chemistry?"

"Ohh, yes." Cynthia inhaled rapturously over her

drink and took a long swallow. "I locked eyes with a guy in the art museum one day last winter and nearly dragged him home."

Allegra sighed longingly and pushed her lens-free purple accessory glasses up her nose. "Me, too, a couple of years ago, at the 'Total Mind And Body Oneness' convention. Believe me, I wanted to make our minds and bodies *totally* one."

"Well..." Missy took a quick sip of her seltzer and blushed. "Remember that guy Brad from our sophomore geology class? Allegra, I don't think you were in that class, but Tracy was. Anyway, my stomach almost dropped out first time I saw him. I still think about him sometimes."

"It happened to me. Just now, on the beach." Tracy half-turned away, her body thrilling again from the memory. "I got something in my contact and when I looked up, he was right there. I almost hyperventilated."

"I see." Cynthia patted back her already smooth hair. "So what are you going to do about it?"

Tracy suppressed a surge of irritation. Cynthia didn't believe there was any mystery to the world. Just challenges and their appropriate solutions. "What did *you* do in the art museum?" She turned to include Allegra and Missy in the question. "At the convention, in biology class?"

Variously mumbled "nothings" came at her from around the deck. Tracy scrubbed her fingers through her short curly hair. "It's ridiculous. None of the guys I've dated made me feel half of what this guy did with one look. A total stranger. And I didn't feel like I could do anything about it."

Cynthia impaled Tracy with the gaze that probably made her business adversaries long for their mommies. "Why not?"

"Why didn't *you?*"

"The same wimpy reason you didn't—all the 'what ifs.'" Allegra pushed back her brightly patterned shawl and started counting on her fingers. "What if he's married, what if he's gay, what if he hates me, what if I imagined the whole thing—"

"What if he's an ex-con, child-molesting, foot-fetishist serial killer?" Missy shuddered. "Or a Republican."

Cynthia bristled. "What's wrong with being—"

"Okay, okay, you two." Allegra reached over and patted Cynthia's and Missy's shoulders, bracelets jangling. "We're talking chemistry, not politics."

"I would have gone after my art museum guy except for the blonde wearing a wedding ring that matched his."

"He was married and he looked at you like that?" Missy's question ended on a squeak of outrage.

"No, no." Tracy shook her head. "It's not a leering look. It's like something inside you is just wired to react to that person. It's something you can't help." She took a long swallow of the vaguely skunky imported beer. "I don't really know what it is. I just know I'll be carrying this guy in my head for days."

"So find him." Cynthia shrugged as if she'd worked out yet another of the world's pressing issues with a snap of her perfectly manicured fingers. "Get out there and find him."

Tracy rolled her eyes. "What, go running after him up the beach?"

"This is a small community. Ask around. Start right here at the party. A lot of the people seem to have been coming to Fish Creek for years. See what you can come up with."

"I don't know." Missy consulted her soda doubtfully. "It could be dangerous tracking down someone you don't know."

"You devour the personal ads every day, what's the difference?" Cynthia sent Missy a teasing smile. "At least Tracy's already attracted to the guy, which is more than you know from 'likes walks by the lake and quiet evenings at home.'"

Missy blushed. "Okay, so I read them. But I would never *answer* one."

"I think Tracy should get off her fanny 'n go for it." Cynthia slapped her thigh, alcohol bringing out the North Carolina accent she usually suppressed.

Allegra nodded eagerly. "What could it hurt to ask around? We could all help. Even if we manage to find out who he is, it doesn't mean you *have* to do anything."

Tracy bit her lip. It was tempting. It was certainly tempting. She'd been dateless for several months, and though she refused to judge her worth as a person in terms of men, the fact remained she wouldn't mind a romantic attachment, especially with someone who didn't spring fully trust-funded out of her Dad's social register. Someone she could spend casual, relaxed time with and forget she'd been thrust into this strange new world of wealth.

She glanced around at her friends. The three women watched her expectantly—Cynthia challenging, Allegra encouraging, Missy apprehensive. Anticipation hung over the trio as if Tracy were being empowered to do something all three women wished they could share in.

All at once, a crazy, fabulous idea sprang into her head. Why couldn't they? She could take up the challenge herself then slap it right back at them.

"I'll do it on one condition." She smiled and fingered the blue foil label on her beer. "That whenever this kind of instant attraction happens to any of us again, we'll pursue the guy."

"Ha!" Cynthia clapped her hands together and laughed, a flush rising attractively up her cheeks. "Great idea, Tracy."

"Wow." Allegra's eyes shot open wide. "Double wow."

"But what if...I mean, I couldn't do this. I'd be horrible at it, I know." Missy bit her lip, looking as if she'd been asked to French kiss a tarantula.

"I could help you out, honey. You'd do fine." Cynthia lowered her voice to a gentle drawl. "Your whole mystique is that you're totally unaware of your attractiveness. Guys love that, I'm serious. And they're not too upset either by your enormous—"

"*Cynthia!*" Missy wrapped her arms across her

chest, trying hard to look outraged over the smile tugging her lips.

"Allegra?" Tracy turned to her old friend and freshman-year roommate, brimming with excitement she hadn't felt since before her mom died.

"Why the heck not?" Allegra shrugged, making her jewelry chime. "I guess at its worst, it would be merely another episode of Allegra's Adventures in Rejection. So I'm in."

"Missy?"

"I…I…" Missy looked at each woman in turn, obviously experiencing the panic of facing certain surrender. "Once we get them, then what?"

"Think of it as science, Missy." Allegra peered over the tops of her glasses with a fierce scholarly expression. "An experiment involving the chemical reaction of female to male."

"Is it merely an animal reaction?" Tracy donned an equally academic scowl. "Or a sign of deeper linkage?"

"In other words," Cynthia gave Missy a sultry smile, "do we fall in love or just get lucky?"

"Oh!" Missy gasped out.

Tracy sent Cynthia a warning scowl. "Missy, you have to admit it would be intriguing. To find out whether these men turn out to be soul mates, life mates, or—"

"Bedmates." Cynthia waggled her eyebrows. "I came, I saw, I conquered, I came again."

"Cynthia, you're incorrigible." Missy clucked her tongue and smiled at the co-worker she'd adopted into their group of University of Wisconsin roommates.

"But would you love me any other way?"

"So it's a deal." Tracy laughed, feeling as if the world was suddenly bright and full of fabulous possibilities. Chances were nothing would come of this encounter. What were the odds someone at the party would be able to identify her mystery man by a vague description? But the high of seeing him, of deciding to take matters into her own hands, was worth it already.

"What should we call ourselves?" Allegra asked. "We should have some kind of name, just for fun."

"Absolutely." Cynthia nodded. "Like those secret clubs I used to organize in grade school that had me as the president and only member."

"I did that, too!" Allegra giggled. "You can't get much more secret than that."

"I've got it." Tracy put down her beer and held up her hands to sketch a giant marquee in the air. "The Manhunters."

Cynthia pretended to choke on her drink. "Manhunters! It's dreadful. I love it."

"Tacky in the extreme." Allegra grinned. "I love it, too."

They turned to look at Missy, who squirmed and made a face. "It's not very scientific. More...predatory."

"Exactly." Tracy lifted her drink for a toast; Cynthia's shot up alongside, then Allegra's; Missy's rose weakly. "To the newly formed Manhunters Club." Tracy smiled, imagining herself introducing Mr. Scruffy to her horrified father, imagining them living happily ever after without a luxury trapping in sight.

"Let all males between the ages of twenty-five and forty, who are straight, single, attractive, financially and mentally sound, non-reliant-on-their-mothers and dying-to-be-in-a-committed-relationship...beware. We, the members of the—"

"Uh, Tracy?" Missy stared past them off the deck, eyes wide, blush rising up her face again. "Was he wearing gray shorts and a white T-shirt?"

Tracy inhaled sharply and clutched her beer. "Yes..."

"Well, well." Cynthia put her hands to her hips and smiled admiringly past Tracy's shoulder. "You sure know how to pick 'em. Go to it, huntress."

Tracy swallowed over what felt like her entire throat congealed into one enormous tight mass and turned around.

There, jogging effortlessly toward them, sunglasses in place, a vee of sweat sticking his shirt to his broad chest, was Manhunter Tracy Richards's very first prey.

2

PAUL SANDERS tried keeping his eyes straight ahead. Tried concentrating on his stride, on the punishing pull of sand at his feet, on the good clean high of physical exercise. Tried doing anything but looking back over at the Richardses' house. He'd gone jogging on this beach on purpose, just to scope out the elegant lakeside bungalow. Just to get a feel for his target.

Derek Richards, self-made multimillionaire, who'd developed the world's first pitless avocado, the world's first banana that stayed at peak ripeness for a week without turning brown, and now, rumor had it, an easy peel seedless tomato that ripened on the vine and didn't rot after picking. Rumor also had it that he'd had a falling-out with Stauderman, Shifrin and Luz. That he'd be looking for a new advertising agency.

Paul Sanders, president and CEO of The Word, Inc., wanted that account. He wanted it bad. The Word, Inc. and Paul himself, had made a promising beginning with the successful ad campaign for Attitude! clothes. Now, poised for the real big time, he was ready to dive in, leave his childhood of poverty far behind him.

He'd done his homework carefully, researched whatever information was out there on Derek Richards's rapid rise from farmer and botanist to celebrated pioneer in food engineering, darling of chain supermarkets and top chefs alike. Since Paul recently bought a summer house only a few hundred yards away, the chance to see the man in his element while remaining incognito had been all too tempting.

Instead, Paul had rushed unnecessarily to aid a woman who turned out to be Derek's daughter—Tracy, wasn't it?—locked eyes with her and fallen prey to the hottest surge of electric desire he could remember in his thirty-one years—not that he'd had too many hot electric surges of desire for the first twelve or so. This unexpected meeting wasn't part of his plan.

The Richardses' house came up slowly on his right. *Damn.* He could see her out on the deck, even in peripheral vision, not that he needed to see her to remember what she looked like. Dark hair curling around fair skin. Lips of a tempting rose color and sexy shape. Loose dress with a blue flowery pattern that clung to her slender figure when the warm breeze blew. A combination of sensuality and innocence, strength and vulnerability that intrigued him beyond the obvious rush of lust. Figured he'd meet someone like that looking like the disadvantaged slob he used to be.

Paul frowned and quelled the irrational wistfulness. Of course it didn't matter. If he—*when* he got the account, he could meet her as who he had become—successful, well-dressed, a man of means, someone who could really impress her. She'd never connect him with the bum who'd been worried about sand in her contacts.

Right now he just had to jog by and resist the urge to turn and look at her again.

He drew even with the house. Was he imagining it or had all the women on the deck lined up to stare at him as he went by?

"Excuse me."

He kept going, ignored the barely audible call. What the hell could she want from him? From the corner of his eye he saw the women scooting down the long deck, following his progress. This was nuts.

"Excuse me." Louder this time. He couldn't pretend he hadn't heard.

Against his better instinct, he stopped. "Yes?"

Four women in summery cocktail dresses, cool and elegant in spite of the heat. A tall, striking brunette, a sweet-faced blonde, a short, frizzy-haired eccentric-looking woman...and her. His eyes found hers instinctively; he felt the same jolt, the same electric pull.

Until he noticed her neighbor, the tall brunette, smirking and jabbing her with her elbow. He put his hands on his hips, overwhelmingly conscious of his sweaty, disheveled appearance.

"Hi." She pushed a curl behind her ear and flashed a warning glance at her neighbor. "I'm...Tracy."

He nodded, wary as all hell, and pitched his voice into a gruff gravelly bass, as if he were recovering from laryngitis. "Hi, Tracy."

A gust of hot wind off the lake hit his back and ruffled the folds of her skirt. The sweet blonde blushed, ducked her head and examined her drink; the frizzy-haired one regarded him frankly over the tops of her bright purple glasses, mouth curved in a know-it-all smile.

Tracy received another jab to the ribs from the tall brunette who was still smirking into her martini glass. He got the distinct impression they were very amused by something. Like him. Four rich girls who couldn't resist playing with the forbidden bad boy. He itched for them to see him in the office, in action, totally on their level. Right now he felt the way he did when Deke Zuzman and his gang of preppies cornered him in the school parking lot at Brookline High and made fun of the clothes his mom bought from a charity store in Roxbury.

"I...was wondering." Tracy started a smile, then bit her lip as if she were trying to suppress it. "If... If... If—"

The tall brunette emitted a barely concealed snort of laughter and turned away. Ms. Frizzy had to cough suddenly; the blonde shot them both a dirty look and jerked her head toward the door. The three of them started backing quietly into the house.

"If what?"

"—if you wanted to come. I mean come *up* and...join me...our...the party."

The female trio ducked into the house, barely suppressing their laughter. Tracy let out a nervous giggle and covered her mouth with her hand, watching him over the top of her fingers.

His attraction dissipated; a slow boil began instead. What fun. Invite the sweaty lowlife hunk of beef up to your swanky party. Have him pass the *hors d'oeuvres.*

Maybe ask him to strip so the guests can get a really good look at the merchandise. Tracy Richards ought to know better. She'd grown up on a farm with barely enough to go around.

Money really changed people. Thank God it hadn't changed him.

"I don't think so, thanks." He turned to walk away when a glimpse of her eyes stopped him. Disappointment. Embarrassment. Not the eyes of a spoiled girl who didn't get what she wanted and was about to scream to Daddy for it.

She opened her mouth to say something when the door to the deck swooshed open and a man came out, mid-thirties, thinning hair, expensive suit.

"Hey, Tracy, why aren't you inside? The party's in full swing." The man stood possessively close to her and glanced down at Paul. "Hey, how are you. Tracy, come on back in. It's hot out here."

He took her arm and tried to turn her. Paul took an instinctive step forward, not at all liking the way the guy touched her, then stepped back. This was none of his business. Maybe Little Miss Megabucks loved being manhandled.

Tracy shook loose and clutched the deck railing, distaste written all over her face. "I'm fine, Jake."

"Okay. We'll bring the party out here, then." Jake glanced again at Paul. "You know this guy, Tracy?"

He asked as if he was curious about something that had washed up on the beach after a sewer overflow day. Paul clenched the hands on his hips, wishing he could ram his balance sheet down Yuppie Boy's throat.

"I...just met him."

"Oh." Jake smiled in obvious relief. "I thought he might be one of your...you know...*friends*."

His tone was smarmy, insinuating. Paul gritted his teeth, surprised at a twinge of disappointment. So he'd pegged her correctly. She collected guys from the wrong side of the tracks for recreational purposes. *Friends,* Jake called them. How delicate. But wealthy women were into that. The whole affair-with-the-tennis-pro dynamic.

"Tracy?" The screen door to the deck whooshed open again. "Why are you out here in this heat, honey? The guests are asking about you."

Paul came to sudden attention. There he was. Balding, mustachioed, slightly overweight, just like his pictures. Derek Richards. The man who could make all of Paul's dreams come true if Paul took the right steps to hook him. But not here, not dressed like this, wanting to strangle and ravish his daughter at the same time.

Mr. Richards caught sight of him and squinted over the railing into the dimming evening light. "Who's this?"

"Dad, this is..." Tracy turned to Paul, eyebrows raised in a question.

"I'm...Dan." He blurted the first name that came into his head.

"Dan." She nodded, not taking her eyes from his.

He returned her gaze, struck again by the way it got inside him and scrambled him up, made him want to hang around when every shred of common sense told him to get the hell away from her, and more to the point, away from her father before "Dan" made any kind of impression Mr. Richards could recall when Paul began vying for his account.

"Dan glad to meet you." Jake chuckled heartily. "Get it?"

"No." Paul and Tracy spoke the word together.

"As in, 'damn glad to meet you'...Dan...damn." Silence reigned on the deck. "Okay. Dan, my man, why don't you come up and join us, then?"

Jake's voice was overly hearty, the invitation too tremendously sincere, the challenge cold and obvious. Mr. Richards gave Jake a surprised look that changed into a thoughtful smile when Jake threw him a wink. Tracy just stared at Paul like he was the biggest present under the tree and if she had anything to say about it, her name would be written all over the tag.

Paul's body went rigid; his tough kid attitude surged to life as if he'd been transported back in time. So the Richards *et al* wanted a lowlife sloppy hunk to amuse them for the evening? He could do that. He could do that so well they wouldn't have a clue who he really was. And one of these days he'd have them eating out of a feedbag he'd have the pleasure of strapping on personally.

"Thanks." He let a slow, make-my-day grin spread over his face. "I'd love to join you."

TRACY CLUTCHED her second beer and watched through narrowed eyes from across the room as Dan reduced Missy and Allegra to near tears and sympathetic clucks with another hard-luck tale. This Manhunters thing wasn't going quite the way she envisioned it. He was supposed to be as enticing a person as he was a physical specimen. He should have the power to attract her mind as well as her body. But he couldn't seem to get over the fact that he didn't have as much money as the other people in the room.

Who the hell cared but him? And maybe Jake. Tracy and her family had done without for decades. The family had been close and united—the Richards vs. Old Man Poverty. They'd had enough, barely, and they'd had their dream of making it big with the produce her dad worked so hard to develop. Now, with the battle won, her mom gone, her dad charging ahead full speed to fill the emptiness, Tracy had lost that first real flush of enjoyment building 21st Century Produce into a success. How much more success did you need when you'd already achieved it? But obviously for this Dan guy, money was the root of all envy.

"Had your chat with poor boy yet?" Cynthia sidled up next to Tracy. "Anything going to happen between you?"

"I doubt it." Tracy jerked her head toward Dan, who didn't seem to want to take off his sunglasses, even indoors. He was putting his hand to his chest, in the middle of some poignant story or other. Allegra gasped; Missy laid a comforting hand on his arm. Her parents' friend Mrs. Teamon, sporting a Caroline Ferrera dress and a seductive aura, joined the group and pointedly introduced herself to him.

"What do you think?"

"Hmph." Cynthia slugged back a sip of her third

martini, characteristically steady as stone in spite of her consumption. Only the southern drawl gave her away. "I think there's something cheesy in the State of Wisconsin."

"That's what I thought, too." Tracy turned toward her friend, who'd grown up a have-not in rural North Carolina. "He's trying awfully hard not to fit in. What did he tell you?"

"Oh, the usual. Lead paint chips and rusty water and food stamps and teenage gangs and gee, wow, isn't this a nice home, gee, wow, I'd like to live in a nice place like this someday, *et cetera...et cetera.*" She waved her hand off to one side. "Made me wish I'd brought a violin."

Tracy gave a wry grin. "Too bad it isn't snowing. We could have him stand outside and sell matches."

The two women turned back to watch Dan in action. He was shaking his head gravely, making Allegra bite her lip. A tear rolled down Missy's cheek. Mrs. Teamon blinked away moisture and called over two of her gold, silk and diamond-accessoried friends.

Tracy tipped her head close to Cynthia. "Think he's full of it?"

"Stuffed to the brim." Cynthia took a swallow of martini and smacked her lips. "Chip on his shoulder the size of Mt. Saint Helens before the explosion."

"Bummer." Tracy sighed. "He's so gorgeous. And he has this amazing intensity about him. Like he gets up and solves world crises before breakfast."

"Bet he's dynamite in the sack, too." Cynthia smacked her lips again, but without drinking this time.

"Why don't you get him alone and find out what his real deal is?"

Another extremely female woman joined the circle around Dan. Tracy gave a wistful shrug that she didn't know was going to be wistful until she shrugged it. Despite his strange behavior, he was still the most attractive man she'd met in a long time, if ever. "Looks like I'm last in line."

"Details, details. Let the expert handle it. I know how you can get him alone, no problem."

"Oh?" Tracy turned and folded her arms across her chest, trying not to show her ridiculous rush of eagerness. "One of your nice subtle methods, Cynthia? March up to him and say, 'hey, buddy, wanna get cozy?'"

Cynthia fixed her with a disdainful stare. "Ha. Ha. Ha. Much better than that. Go outside on the deck."

"And...?"

"And stand there. Let the breeze blow your dress around, lift your head dreamily toward the stars, shake your hair sensually in the moonlight and look lonely and available. If he's interested, he'll come out."

"Ha! More likely Jake will come out and breathe scotch fumes down my neck."

"I'll take care of Jake." Cynthia tossed back the rest of her martini and patted her hair. "He won't know what hit him. Oh, and by the way, when you walk past Dan's harem if you can make 'by-accident' eye contact, so much the better."

Tracy laughed. "Cynthia, you are a master."

"Uh-huh." Cynthia looked around and gave Tracy a

gentle shove toward the door. "Get going, incoming puppy love. *Jake!* Over here, sugar! Can you help me? I really need some good male advice...."

Tracy moved away, past a few annoyed husbands making snide remarks about the sloppy intruder, and pulled even with the gaggle of females cooing over Dan's latest tale of woe. She slowed her steps, feeling completely ridiculous. He had about ten dozen adoring women all over him, why the hell would he glance over at her?

He did. Raised his head in the middle of a sentence and caught her eye, as if he knew she'd be there, as if he'd been keeping track of where she was in the room. She jerked her eyes away and walked out into the humid air of the deck, closing the door carefully behind her, wondering who had taken away her ability to breathe naturally, who had poured warmth all through her body.

She clutched the railing and forced her lungs to operate. This attraction was so real, so powerful, she could suddenly understand why people got involved with someone totally wrong for them, a practice she'd always found bewildering. Right now she wanted to throw Dan in the sand and ride him like a cowgirl. She couldn't recall ever feeling this...bestial about wanting a man. Potent stuff. Dangerous. Exciting.

The door to the deck slid open behind her. Tracy's body became a stiff block of receptive nerve endings. She had to force herself to relax, to lift her head dreamily toward the stars, which were unfortunately hidden by clouds. She tried to shake her hair sensually in the barely visible white glow of moonlight—except her hair was too short to do more than wiggle—and attempted to look lonely and available, which was hardest since she was ready to scream wanting to turn around and see if it was him.

"Hi."

Tracy closed her eyes and let his deep raspy voice run through her. *Oh God. It was him.* He leaned on the railing next to her, his presence so powerful she nearly wanted to run away from it.

Nearly. "Enjoying the party?"

"You have nice friends."

"There are a few men in there, too, would you believe." She winced. What a stupid jealous-sounding thing to say.

He chuckled. "You coulda fooled me."

The deck door slid open a few inches; whoever was opening it paused to talk to another guest, his hand still on the door, on his way out. *Oh, no.* Was it Jake? Had Cynthia not managed to delay him? Had someone—

"Want to take a walk?"

Tracy's head snapped toward Dan. A walk? In the dark? On a near-empty beach with the most attractive man she'd ever encountered? Gee, she'd have to think about that one for at least— "Okay."

She led the way down to the beach, telling herself not to get carried away. Reminding herself that something wasn't quite right about him. Maybe as Cynthia said, he had a chip on his shoulder about wealthy people. Or maybe he was a con man who preyed on rich, lonely women by gaining their sympathy. Tracy wrinkled her nose. Rich lonely women always sounded like such a pathetic way to be female, except that it happened to describe her to a tee.

Of course he could also be some psycho Door County Strangler type, but it wasn't likely. If only he'd take off the dark glasses she might be able to sense more about who he was.

"Nice night."

"Mm-hmm." But then walking on the beach alone with him could make a blizzard a nice night. "I'm glad you decided to come to the party. It was impulsive of me to invite you. I don't usually pounce on strangers."

"Oh?" He sounded surprised, as if he thought she was a professional stranger pouncer. "Why me?"

Tracy's eyes shot open and froze that way. Uh. How did one answer politely that the sight of him turned her into a depraved beast woman? "Oh...I'm...not really sure."

"Well here's a guess." His voice didn't change much from its gravelly tone, but she thought she could detect a hint of bitterness. "You wanted to amuse your friends and relations with someone who never puts radicchio in his salad?"

Tracy stopped walking. "Is that what you thought?"

"I wondered."

"Oh, my God, not at *all*." She could have laughed at the irony. She was probably the last person on the earth to think financial hardship was amusing.

He stepped back toward her. "Jake and your dad seemed to think I was pretty funny."

"Yes, well, they have strange senses of humor. Dad's okay, he's just one of those brilliant people who's also a little clueless. Jake's a snob."

"He seems to think highly of you."

"He thinks highly of my income bracket." Her turn to sound bitter.

Dan took a step closer at the same time the moon hit a thinner patch of clouds and brightened the humid air around them so she could more clearly see the lines of his face, blurred by the days-old beard, and the shiny glint of light off his lenses.

"Why do you still have on your glasses?" She was dying to see his eyes. In her fantasy they were blue and deep and you could lose yourself in them for hours at a time.

"Prescription. I broke my other ones. Can't see a thing without them. You still haven't answered my question, Tracy."

"Oh?" Her voice came out breathless and silly into the warm still air around them. "What question was that?"

"Why you invited me to the party."

"Oh. That question." *Because you made me crazy with lust and I swore an oath to my friends that I would hunt you down.* "Well...I just thought...you might—"

He focussed on her so intently she could imagine his gaze burning through the glasses. "Was it because of the chemistry between us when we first saw each other?"

Tracy's mouth opened and closed several times. Luckily she produced no sound, because if she had, she probably would have said something like, *"Hamnadgjwek."*

"I didn't mean to embarrass you." He grinned and started walking again, his movements easy and graceful, as if he were totally comfortable being in his own skin. "You don't have to answer."

Tracy followed, stumbling on nonexistent obstacles in the sand, her movements shaky and off-balance, which pretty much mirrored the state of her brain. She'd told herself not to get carried away by the romance of the moment. Her mission was to find out about Dan. If he checked out okay, if he wasn't just faking the poor-boy thing for some questionable reason or other, *then* she could get carried away by the romance of the moment.

"So where did you grow up?" she asked.

"Boston. Roxbury, actually. Mom put Dad through Tufts Medical School, Dad said 'thanks, seeya later,' married some Beacon Hill society chick. Mom raised me cleaning people's homes. I came to Wisconsin because my grandmother lives in Wauwatosa and Mom moved back here to be close to her. The end." He punctuated the story with gestures and ended dropping his hands to his side.

"Oh, gosh." No dramatic bid for sympathy there, but Tracy brimmed with it anyway. His dry recital of facts touched her more deeply than if he'd tried ranking his childhood with the world's great tragedies as he had at the party. Possibly he'd only been trying to put one over on the clucking brood surrounding him. Possibly he was being straight with her. She had to admit she really liked that idea. Especially if the reason behind it was that he liked her. That she sparked something inside him the way he did in her.

"So what's a nice guy like you doing in a neighborhood like this?"

He chuckled. "Interesting perspective. I work for the Gabriels on Apple Lane. Handyman, pool boy, whatever you want to call me. They need it done, I do it."

"Oh." She chided herself for her disappointment. Now who was a snob? So he wasn't ambitious, that didn't make him less of a person. He certainly seemed intelligent. Maybe he had some other goal he was working toward at the same time. "Have you...been doing that for a while?"

"Not long."

"Are you planning to stay with them?"

"What, you don't think I can fulfill my every dream cleaning the Gabriels' pool?"

She heard the smile in his voice and laughed her relief. "Maybe, I don't know you. But my guess would be that you have something else going."

"Why?"

"Just a hunch."

"And if I don't?" He stopped and turned toward her with an abruptness that made her rear back. "If I'm determined to be a pool boy for the rest of my life would you think less of me? Or more?"

Tracy studied him curiously; his brows were raised, lips curved in a half smile, but his jaw was set and that potent intensity radiated from his body. She really really wanted to see his eyes. "I'm sorry. I don't understand."

"Would I be more attractive to you the way I am now, or in a suit at the head of a corporate table?" His lips returned to the stiff half smile as if her answer would make up his mind about her.

Luckily, she could answer honestly and ease any worry he might have on that score. "I prefer you the way you are."

"That's what I thought."

She frowned. Something about the way he said that didn't make it sound like a compliment. "Why do I get the feeling that's a mark against me?"

"Let's put it this way." He stepped closer, the nearness of his body making the wide expanse of beach seem like an intimate enclosed space. "*Now* you have to answer."

She gaped at him, flushed, disoriented, desire buzzing wildly through her. "Answer what?"

"Whether you felt the chemistry between us when we met."

Her breath came in a long inhaled rush. She knew how she'd answer. And she knew where her answer would lead them. "Yes," she whispered.

"I told you whatever the Gabriels need, I do." He reached out, trailed a finger up her bare arm to her shoulder, over the line of her collarbone to her cheek. The bitterness was back in his tone, along with a barely perceptible dose of sarcasm. "I'm thinking you're looking to have me service your needs as well. Uncomplicated guy, uncomplicated sex. Am I right?"

Tracy stiffened. He thought she preferred him scruffy because she wanted him for some kind of trans-socioeconomic screwing? Obviously he had her confused with Mrs. Teamon's gang of boy-raiders. And she'd been stupid and naive enough to think he really liked her.

Colossal, major mistake.

Her disappointment brought tears perilously close to the surface; she stuffed them back down under a nice healthy coating of fury. The jerk. He'd been playing her all night, playing all of them. He was a worse snob than Jake, not able to see past their money. Well, she could play, too. They could make it a nice unpleasant round of doubles.

"Oh, Dan." She forced her body to relax, turned her face so his finger brushed her lips. "I'm so glad you understand. That's exactly what I want you for. To service my needs."

"That's what I thought." The words came out hard, clipped.

"And...oh!" She gave a tiny gasp. "I have a very pressing need right now."

"I just bet you do." Harder. More clipped. He sounded like he wanted to throw her in the lake.

"I want you, Dan. I need you." She leaned toward him and ran her tongue over her lips, enjoying herself hugely. "...to clean our pool."

3

PAUL WIPED OFF the last traces of shaving cream with his monogrammed gray towel and hung it carefully back on the brass towel warmer in the corner of his bathroom. He slapped on some *Route du Thé* cologne from Barney's, New York, combed his newly short hair and grinned, feet moving to the beat of an Oscar Peterson CD. Today was the day.

Today he would trot into the Richardses' empire and show them he was their man. That he was capable of coming up with a campaign that would take those peel-easy, seedless tomatoes and bring the world to its knees wanting them. That he could produce a slick, fabulous sales tool combining sizzle with the more obvious down-home charm of a family business made good. A tool that would put The Word, Inc. on the map and solidify Paul's fortunes.

Not to mention get a little of his own back from a certain woman who'd delivered one of the most stinging put-downs he'd ever experienced. Growing up in inner city Boston, being bussed into a wealthy suburban school system and surviving its special brand of elitist cruelty, he'd thought his skin was tough enough to make a covering for the space shuttle.

But Tracy Richards had managed to hurt him. First

by making him want her so badly he nearly threw her down in the sand in spite of his contempt for her trophy-hunting attitude towards him, then again by rejecting him for the very reason he attracted her in the first place—his apparent lack of social station. Well she could kiss his...ad campaign.

He strutted naked through the bedroom accompanied by one of Ed Thigpen's rousing percussion solos and opened the door to his immense walk-in closet to select his outfit. One Thomas Pink custom-made shirt. One Brioni suit. Hermès necktie. Tse cashmere socks. Prada shoes. Breitling watch.

There. He nodded to his reflection in the full-length mirror behind the closet door and played air bass along with Ray Brown. Goodbye Dan the Pool Boy. Hello Paul Sanders, CEO. He'd meet the Richards again on an entirely new level, enjoy their respect, interact with them and deliver a fabulous pitch for his company that would knock the competition flat, while Tracy and her dad had no clue he was the same bum who'd crashed their party a few weeks ago.

He opened the portfolio he'd brought home with him to check the presentation, fingers playing a mean piano along with Oscar. Nothing could be left to chance on this one. No room for mistakes, boards out of order, sloppy slipups. What he chose to leave out in high-tech dazzle for the team's pitch, he made up for with professionalism, not to mention quality. Attitude! clothes. Grime-Away industrial cleaner. Magnet-Magic kids' toys. All successful, all impressive. They'd better be. The Richards could afford to fly in big advertising guns from N.Y. and L.A. He'd be competing against the best.

The apartment buzzer rang in the staccato rhythm that let him know his friend and neighbor Dave was at the door.

"Come in." He shot open the deadbolt and boogied back to the boards, leaving Dave to stroll in by himself.

"Hey, Colonel." Dave sauntered in, turned down Oscar from the deafening blare Paul loved to a more ear-friendly level and fell back onto Paul's couch. Dave had a trust fund the size of Fort Knox, so his movements were rarely hampered by anything like regular employment hours. "Today's the day, huh? Going for the Richardses' account?"

"Yup." Paul glanced at his watch and closed the portfolio. "Two hours and forty-two minutes from now I'll be on."

"Will *she* be there?" Dave picked up a Tiffany's paperweight from the coffee table and started turning it over and over in his huge hands. "Your girlfriend?"

Paul sent over a look of disgust. "Yes, *she* will be there. And she's not my girlfriend."

"Yet."

Paul shrugged, playing percussion, trying to look unconcerned, unaffected and un—anything. As much as he was looking forward to getting some pride back, he hadn't been able to stop thinking about Tracy in ways that had nothing to do with revenge. One fantasy in particular had evolved entirely against his will from a picture of her on her knees, begging forgiveness, to a picture of her on her knees doing something a hell of a lot more enticing than begging.

"I'm telling you, it's only a matter of time."

Paul banished the picture and played two huge final chords on his drafting table as the song ended. "Until what?"

"Until you're in her pants."

Paul chuckled and shook his head. "You know it's a good thing none of your conquests ever hear you talk like that."

"Huh?" Dave put on a look of utter who-me? innocence that dissolved into a hearty grin. "Speaking of which, we're overdue for a night out. All work and no sex make Paul and Dave dull boys. Cindee Dee Morrison called me yesterday and says her cousin will be in town next weekend."

"Cindee Dee? The one who thought being Homo sapien meant you liked boys?"

"That's her." Dave put down the paperweight and lay back on the couch, hands cupped behind his head, gazing dreamily at the ceiling. "Cindee Dee Cup. Her cousin is twenty-two and doesn't know the meaning of—"

"Pretty much anything?" Paul winced. "No offense, Dave, but I wouldn't mind spending time with some women who don't think college is something you make with paste and magazine pictures."

Dave turned his head with a "gotcha" expression on his handsome face. "You mean like Tracy?"

"What does she have to do with it?" A distinctly defensive tone crept into his voice and he tried to filter it out.

"Only everything." Dave heaved his enormous frame to a sitting position on Paul's sofa. "You haven't been the same since you met her. You're obsessed. I think this is It. The One. I told you it would hit you like that someday. I may be next, who knows?"

"Oh, come on." Paul smacked his palm down on the table. "The woman is a shallow man-eating nightmare who toys with men not as well off as she is. Or no, let me be corrected, as well off as she has *become*."

"Okay, let me get this straight. She meets guys that she's attracted to, who are attracted to her, and she has sex with them and they both have a really great time and that's bad because..."

"It's the principle of the thing, Dave." Paul zipped up his portfolio with sharp jerky movements. Life to Dave was incredibly simple. With his money, he'd always been able to do exactly as he pleased exactly when he pleased. He couldn't seem to understand that most people weren't that lucky. Most people couldn't blithely preach that wealth wasn't important, that people should rise above it, while they needed two hands to count their own millions. "She's attracted to them just because they don't have any money. It has nothing to do with who they are."

"You like brunettes, right? Petite ones, slender, long legs, small boobs?"

"Yeah?"

"So she likes poor guys, what's the difference?"

"The difference is—" Paul rolled his eyes. Dave's

logic was so whacked, you couldn't even argue against it. "She assumed because of my clothes I was nothing but an infinitely available sex machine."

"You called?" Dave winked, got off the couch and stretched. "Okay, okay, I'm not going to fight. I never met the woman. She might be as awful as you say. But when it hits you that hard you gotta pay attention, that's all. Me, I've never been hit that hard. But someday I will be. And you can bet my first move isn't going to be for revenge."

Paul picked up his portfolio and headed for the door. "I don't think of it as revenge. I think of it as instructional justice. I'll show her what a charming, sophisticated, intelligent guy I am," he grinned at Dave's raised eyebrow, "then when she values me for who I am, not what I'm wearing, I'll let her know who she was talking to last month on the beach."

"If she's into poor guys, what makes you think she'll go for you the way you are now?"

Paul sighed. "Dave. I don't want her to go for me, that's the point. I want her to get to know me, and value me as a fellow human."

"Oh, I get it. *Then* you want her to go for you."

"Read my lips." Paul turned out the lights and gestured out the door. "I. Do. Not. Want. Her. To. Go. For. Me."

"Amazing." Dave clapped a giant hand to his forehead. "I just saw something I've never seen before."

Paul pulled his condo door closed behind them, not in the mood for any more Dave-ian drama. "What's that?"

"You." Dave leaned forward and glared hard into Paul's face. "Completely full of it."

"CLEANLINESS IS NEXT to Modliness!" The gleaming white teeth of the toupéed ad executive from Prestall, Prestall and Prestall stayed visible entirely too long through lips stretched in a cheesy grin. "Our biggest client, and most successful campaign. It brought Mod detergent into houses across America."

Tracy nodded politely, wishing she could drop her head into her hands. His board showed a slovenly woman in a grease-spattered kitchen using a bargain brand to mop her floor, juxtaposed next to a happy fulfilled woman with a house that obviously made bacteria run screaming, effortlessly guiding her Mod-soaked mop around the already-clean linoleum. She'd probably just finished doing the mailman on the kitchen floor and was wiping up the icky traces.

This was after the boards showing women loving their husbands much more once they were handed enormous diamonds. And the man whose entire life took a turn for the better once he bought an expensive all-terrain vehicle big enough for the entire Green Bay Packers team, to commute five city blocks to work. Sometimes she got so sick of the commercialism, she wanted to run away to the farm and hole up there forever.

It was all about money. All about how your life would change, if you just had enough so you could spend and acquire, spend and acquire. Only then would the Happiness Fairy darken your doorstep.

Crap. All of it. 21st Century Produce tomatoes would be an ingenious convenient introduction into the market. They wouldn't save anyone's marriage or self-esteem.

Next.

Mr. Prestall wrapped up his presentation with a flourish. Her father beamed as if he'd been handed his life's desire and ushered the pitch team out of the room. Tracy barely contained a snort of laughter. When her father acted that hearty it meant he was totally disgusted. Thank goodness.

The next company was worse. The team wore red running sneakers and red neckties, burst into the meeting room to a blast of electro-pop music and proceeded to put on a razzle-dazzle show that would put the Oscar ceremonies to shame. Except their ideas were just as overdone and obvious as the presentation. The unattractive in-your-face twenty-something guy selling hamburgers. The TV ads shot with handheld cameras so you got queasy watching. The dot-com company ads that left you wondering what recreational drugs were being passed around when the concept was born. Wasn't anyone in advertising normal?

Her father's manner grew heartier and heartier, his laughter louder. He shook hands all around with the team, beaming, closed the door behind them and rolled his eyes, the smile dropping off his face as if it weighed a ton.

"God, that was awful. Can you imagine? My tomatoes thrown around as if they were the mystical saviors of the universe? Or hawked by young men who need a shave and an attitude adjustment? Dreadful. Your mom would have thrown up."

He moved heavily to the table, sat and wiped a hand across his eyes. Tracy's throat tightened. She leaned forward and gripped his arm in a comforting squeeze, to let him know she was there. As long as he needed her to support him, she'd stay. As much as she felt suffocated in this business at times, it was beyond her to leave him alone with his grief.

Her father patted her hand and cleared his throat, inhaled and summoned a burst of energy.

"The next company shows promise." He pulled the last folder off his pile and opened it. "Relatively new, headed by a local man named Paul Sanders. A real gogetter, very ambitious. His company did the ads for Attitude! clothes."

A jolt went through Tracy's body. The last time she saw the logo for Attitude! it had been printed in a careless scrawl across a T-shirt, clinging to some pretty fabulous musculature.

She pushed the thought away. Her first Manhunter adventure had been a dud. Maybe there'd be others. Or maybe she'd do better forgetting the enticing pull of chemistry and using her brain to choose her next potential date. Dan had turned out to be a Class-A jerk. Manipulative, judgmental, you name it.

Too bad she couldn't get him the hell out of her mind.

Even when she was preparing to zap him with the "clean my pool" line, her body had had many many other ideas. Ideas that still had this habit of intruding into her day, into her thoughts, into her daydreams. Like the one where he got so angry at the pool line, that instead of whirling away and disappearing into the dark night as he actually had, he grabbed her, kissed her with one of those killer I-won't-take-no-for-an-answer kisses that would make her furious in real life, pulled her down onto the sand and tormented her until she was reduced to animal-mating instincts, her body wanting only to—

"Good afternoon, Mr. Richards. I'm Paul Sanders."

Tracy started, brought her eyes back into focus and brought her wanton wayward mind back into the conference room. Paul Sanders. Nice-looking guy. Blond, about six foot, expensively dressed. Young to have his own firm and a big account like Attitude! This guy either came from money or he'd made plenty of it. But after the cheesy old guy and the trying-too-hard trendy one, at least he looked normal.

"Derek Richards." Her father shook his hand, smiling one of his real smiles, glanced at Tracy, then back at Paul. She resisted rolling her eyes. She knew what that glance meant. *Here's another male possibility for you.* "Nice to meet you, Paul. This is my daughter, and 21st Century's vice president, Tracy."

For one surreal moment, Paul Sanders kept his eyes on her father. His smile took on a sort of strained quality she couldn't interpret, then he turned and stepped toward her, hand outstretched. "Hello, Tracy."

Tracy took his hand and shook it, smiled and told him it was nice to meet him.

At least she was pretty sure that's what she was doing. Because she was having another distinctly Manhunter moment, possibly even more powerful than the one with Dan, complete with electric attraction, all-over bodily warmth, and a consuming desire to get naked. His eyes were a fabulous blue with touches of gray and held a strange intensity, gazing into hers as if he were waiting for some kind of judgment.

She stepped back, took her hand out of his, took her seat at the table and busied herself with the top file on the pile in front of her, aware of the stupid blush on her face, aware of her father staring at her curiously.

Oh. My. God. If she wasn't vice president of the company she'd skulk out and hide in the restroom until she could regain touch with reality. This was definitely her month for chemistry.

Paul and his team launched into their presentation. The ideas for their previous clients were brilliant. Sassy or refined, understated or bold, they got hold of the essence of the product, of what made it special in a way that made consumers feel they were being seduced into buying, not badgered.

Tracy could feel her father's mounting excitement in the way he kept changing positions in the chair, tapping his fist against his mouth, mumbling quietly to himself. She tried to stay absorbed in the ads, but her eyes kept focussing on Paul. There was something increasingly familiar about him. About the way he moved, his energy, the way he smiled. But there was no way she'd forget eyes like that; she was sure she'd never seen them before. Did he look like someone she knew? Had she only caught a glimpse of him somewhere? At a party? At a movie? At Sendik's supermarket?

His presentation ended. Her father rose and asked a few pointed questions. Paul stood calmly, legs spread, hands fisted on his hips, pushing back his jacket. Tracy's eyes shot wide. Her breath flew into her mouth.

Dan. A dead ringer for him.

She frowned. How likely was it that she'd feel the same chemical pull from two different guys she happened to meet within a few short weeks of each other who looked exactly the same?

Not.

Thoughts and images started banging around inside her head. The hesitation to join the party. The insistence on being poor. The strange rough voice. The sunglasses that never came off.

Dan was Paul Sanders. And he was trying to put one over on them all. Again.

Her eyes narrowed, her blood worked itself into a nicely vicious boil. Cocky son of a bitch. Pretending to be poor, admiring their wealth, making Tracy out to be some kind of gigolo collector. When all along he had his own successful not-exactly-pool-cleaning business and a closetful of designer labels.

Her eyes narrowed further; her nostrils widened to let out the jets of air her furious lungs were producing. What gall, when he needed their business, to think he could taunt them like that. What nerve, to show up here thinking they wouldn't recognize him just because he dressed better and cut his hair. Did he think they were like *him?* That they couldn't see past the trappings to the real person underneath?

Why that lowlife lying, money-grubbing—

"Tracy?" Her father nudged her with his elbow. "I said did you have any questions?"

Tracy swallowed. Paul was staring at her—was it a trifle apprehensively? Her father was definitely amused. No doubt her dad thought she'd been lost gazing at Paul with unbridled passion.

Well think again, Dad.

"No questions." She kept her tone cool, managed not to blush this time. "Thanks for coming, Mr. Sanders."

"It's Paul." He smiled, and even across the room she had to brace herself against the impact.

"Thanks for coming...Paul." She made her voice even cooler, bent her head over some papers and lifted a hand in a brief wave—the queen dismissing a vassal.

"I'll see you out." Her father escorted Paul out of the room as if he were the returned prodigal son.

The second they disappeared down the hall, Tracy collected her things and banged out of the conference room. Not too hard to see who was getting this job. Apparently Paul's ruse had worked—at least on her father. She barged into her office suite and slammed her files back onto her secretary's desk.

Mia jumped a mile and got the Solitaire game off her computer screen in a big hurry. "So...how did it go?"

"Fine. Splendid. Terrific."

Mia grabbed for the stack of files and busied herself

rearranging them. "Uh...so I guess it's not the greatest time to ask if I can leave early today?"

"Again?"

"I have a date."

"Again?"

"Yeah." Mia blinked her eyes rapidly and tossed back her enormous mass of blond hair. "You remember Tim? The one I dated for awhile after Joe but before Fred? Well this is Tim's new girlfriend's sister's brother-in-law. Frank."

Tracy made a short attempt to figure that one out, then waved her hands in surrender. "Fine. Go. See you tomorrow."

"Thanks, Tracy!" Mia jumped up to her five-foot height and slung her purse over her shoulder. "You're the best boss ever. I got those letters done, they're on your desk. I'll come in early tomorrow to do the filing."

She hurried out and nearly bumped into Tracy's dad as he came into her suite.

"Where's she off to?" Her father frowned over his shoulder.

"She has a date."

Her father frowned harder. "You're too easy on her, Tracy. Your mother and I didn't build this business leaving work at four every day."

"I know, I know. But your goal was to build the business. Hers is to get married. That's what's important to her."

He nodded and crossed her office to stare out the window at Kilbourn Avenue in downtown Milwaukee. "What's important to you, Tracy? What's your goal?"

Tracy gaped at him, but his profile told her nothing. He'd never asked her a question like that, and honestly, she wasn't sure she knew the answer anymore. But she damn well knew what he wanted to hear.

"I want to see 21st Century Produce established as the standard for researching, developing, growing and shipping new vegetable and fruit products."

His eyes narrowed slightly; he nodded, still gazing out the window. "And what about Mia's goal. Don't you want to get married?"

"Someday, sure, if I meet the right person."

He turned abruptly. "What do you think of Paul Sanders?"

Tracy closed her eyes and took a long, slow breath. This had to stop. "Dad, I wish you wouldn't try to foist me onto every single man my age who shows the appropriate bottom line. The man is perfectly attractive, but it's obvious he's totally consumed by ambition and probably completely—"

"I meant professionally. What did you think of the pitch?"

"Oh." Tracy felt a sudden need to become involved in rearranging her pencils. "It was...great."

She said the last word between her teeth because she knew exactly what was going to happen. Her dad would jump all over Paul, because Paul's style was clearly a fabulous match for 21st Century, and then Tracy would have to trip all over Paul every time he visited and force herself not to deliver a well-deserved right hook to the jaw over the Door County incident.

And, okay, force herself not to think about that bruising savage fantasy kiss in the darkness.

"I agree. I think we should go with him." Her father frowned and tapped the sill. "Did he look at all familiar to you?"

Tracy busied herself with some more fascinating pencil maneuvers. Should she tell him? He was obviously so excited about Paul being involved in 21st Century. Truth to tell, the pitch and the quality of ads had her revved up, too. Exposing Paul as "Dan" could ruin all that for her dad. Not exposing him would mean he'd won, at least for now. She needed more time to decide.

"No. Not...particularly." She groaned silently. Hedging was among her worst talents.

"Good. It's just me, then." Her father clapped his hands, apparently unconcerned with her lousy hedge. "I'll call him in a few days and spring the good news. Pretend we had a hard time deciding so he won't think we're easy."

"Good idea." Except he already thought *she* was easy.

Her father strode to the door, more animated than she'd seen him in months. Tracy's heart lifted. Okay, maybe it was worth tripping over Paul/Dan a few times in the next month or so to see her dad looking so much like his old self, to see that enthusiasm returning, the spark—

"Oh, Tracy, by the way." He paused with his hand

on her door. Something twisted warily in her stomach at his carefully casual tone.

"Yes, Dad?"

"You know how important this campaign is to me, how important this product was to your mom."

"Yes."

"I think we should work closely with Paul on all details as his ideas are developed."

"Okay..." Where was this going? He hadn't said anything less than obvious so far.

"I've been wanting to spend some time back up at the farm. I have an idea for a sweet cranberry I'd like to try. We could grow those in-state and handle the production end ourselves."

"Uh..." A voice inside her began to have a pretty good idea where this was going and it was screaming, "no" at the top of its lungs. "...Dad?"

"So I'd like you to be the contact." He grinned entirely too cheerfully. "The one to give Paul everything he needs."

He left her office, not waiting a microsecond for the huge protest that was ready to explode out of her. She choked it back and turned her frustration to her stapler instead, pounding it until little folded bits of metal littered her desk in a bizarre staple snowfall.

She knew enough not to argue. Arguing only cemented her father's positions. The way to change Derek Richards's mind was to chip away at his stand slowly, gather and show evidence over time that his decision had been the wrong one.

There was only one problem.

Tracy slumped onto her desk and rested her head on cool unsympathetic blotting paper, bumpy with staples that would probably leave little red indentations in her forehead. Unless she could think of something fast, the time required to change her father's mind was time she'd have to spend with a money-grubbing, status-worshipping, lying little weasel named Paul Sanders.

4

"TRACY?"

Tracy sank back into her office chair and clenched the receiver against her ear. No question who was on the other end of the line. Only one man's voice had the ability to turn her insides into melted cheese. Damn him. "This is Tracy."

"Paul here, Paul Sanders. Your dad just called me and I wanted to speak to you personally and say how thrilled we are at The Word, Inc. to be awarded this account."

Tracy sneered and rolled her eyes. *Sleazebag.* "I'm so glad."

"I also wanted to say that I'm pleased we'll be—" he cleared his throat, "—working closely together developing this campaign. I actually prefer to have my clients involved every step of the way."

"I see." *Scum-sucking, bottom-dwelling, algae-coated mutant.* "How nice."

"I have my calendar here." The sound of pages flipping came over the line. "We'll have our first brainstorming session early next week. Maybe you'd like to be there? What day is good for you?"

"How about..." *When hell freezes over, when ostriches fly, when Mars bears life, when reality TV shows something real.* "Tuesday? Ten o'clock?"

"We usually do our brainstorming in the evening, when we're more relaxed. How about seven?"

Tracy narrowed her eyes. "Seven. Your office."

"My place."

"Excuse me?"

"Twenty-one eleven North Lake Drive, third floor. It's more relaxing, more conducive to the easy flow of ideas."

More conducive to the easy flow of bull, Liar Boy. "I don't think—"

"My two colleagues will be there, Karen and Jim. We usually have a glass of wine, dim the lights, sit in comfortable chairs and throw out whatever comes to us. The ideas build off each other until we get what we want. It's an amazing process. You'll enjoy it."

Like hell. She gritted her teeth. "Seven. Your place."

"Terrific. It's a date."

Tracy hung up the phone. Oh, no it bloody well wasn't. All the attraction in the world couldn't make time spent with Paul into a date.

She snatched up her briefcase and stalked out of the office, out of the building and to her car. On the short drive to Louise's Italian Café where the Manhunters met every week for dinner, her mood only got fouler. Never in her life had she experienced this torturous combination of lust and fury. Knowing what he was like should have effectively stomped out every last ember of desire. Finding out he was a manipulative, etc., etc., should have triggered her brain to signal a cool-down for the rest of her body. But while half of her very sensibly wanted to dip him in boiling oil, the other half wanted the oil warm and lightly scented, spread with her fingers over his entire body.

Worse, she'd spent the past few days sinking lower and lower into guilty misery watching her dad become more and more enchanted by Paul and his work. The last time she'd lied to her father she'd been twelve years old and blamed a broken window on a neighbor kid. Turned out her dad had seen her line drive heading for the house. He'd given her a sorrowful, "Oh, Tracy" look that had made her writhe in an agony of shame, and had dutifully doled out a this-hurts-me-more-than-it-hurts-you punishment. One month of being grounded and sixteen years of being honest had resulted. Now, unless she broke the news about Paul being Dan, unless she risked bursting the bubble that had lifted Dad's spirits for the first time in so long, that streak of honesty was as good as over.

She grabbed an open parking space on Jackson Street and strode to the restaurant through the thick hot air, reaching the entrance at the same time as a dark, model-gorgeous man, cool and elegant in a perfectly tailored summer suit who opened the door and gallantly gestured her ahead of him. She smiled gratefully into his eyes, praying for a Manhunter moment, then sighed, gave her name to the hostess and went into the welcome coolness of the bar area to wait for her friends.

Nothing. The man was stunning. And probably nice, to boot. Probably didn't pretend to be something he wasn't to get what he wanted from people he didn't respect. And Tracy felt nothing.

Way to bleeping go.

She tried to catch the bartender's eye a few times at the already full bar with no luck. Today, she definitely and rather uncharacteristically needed a stiff one.

It hadn't really sunk in—or maybe she hadn't *let* it sink in—until she made the appointment with Paul today that she was really going to have to deal with him. Really going to have to spend hours at a time in his company. She had to come up with some kind of defense so she wouldn't feel so conflicted. So she could stay cool and confident and untouched and not betray that she was majorly overheated either by anger or...that other thing.

She gestured again to the bartender who seemed to have a blind spot exactly her size and shape. Nothing like feeling invisible to bolster your spirits.

"Hello, hello." Cynthia and Missy arrived from their jobs at Atkeson, Inc. Missy gave Tracy a hug while Cynthia cast an eye around for any interesting male sights.

"What's up with our first Manhunter quest?" Cynthia lifted one manicured forefinger and the bartender charged over with a welcoming smile. "Tanqueray martini, extra dry with a twist, diet cola for Missy and...beer, Tracy?"

"A bourbon Manhattan."

The bartender nodded and walked back to his bottles.

"A Man*hat*tan?" Cynthia raised her eyebrows. "Honey, you better tell us what's going on."

"Is everything okay?" Missy ducked out of the way

of a couple jostling rudely past her and apologized over her shoulder.

"Everything's splendid. Fabulous. Tremendously wonderful." The words came out distorted by Tracy's clenched teeth.

Cynthia and Missy exchanged glances. "Uh-oh. What is—"

"Hey, guys." Allegra emerged from between two smartly dressed women, a riot of color and jangling jewelry. "Sorry I'm late. One of my 'Am I the Me I Want to Be?' students achieved nirvana and had to tell me about it."

"Nirvana?" Missy frowned. "What *is* that exactly?"

Cynthia retrieved their drinks from the bartender and ordered Allegra a sparkling water. "Nirvana? Isn't that like a state of constant orgasm?"

A business-suited bar patron did a double take toward her; Cynthia smiled sweetly. "Yes, you heard me. Ever been there?"

The man's mouth fell open; his date jerked his attention back before he could answer.

"*Cynthia.*" Missy grabbed her arm. "We were trying to find out what was wrong with Tracy."

"Something's wrong?" Allegra peered at her over the tops of her plain-glass black granny glasses, her hair a brassy red bob today. "You do look a little out of optimal balance. What's up?"

"It's Paul."

"Paul?" The three women stared blankly.

"Paul Sanders, CEO of The Word, Inc. advertising agency, brimming with wealth and good taste, the newly hired advert man for 21st Century Produce's latest product..." Tracy narrowed her eyes, preparing for the killer punch line. "Also known as Dan the mysterious sunglassed Door County beach bum."

The women's gasps and subsequent looks of outrage did a lot for Tracy's frazzled nerves. Nothing like allies to make troubles less overwhelming. If anyone could help her figure out what to do, her friends could.

"The same man?" Missy's face crumpled in horror. "But he was so *nice.* And those sad stories about his childhood..."

"One-hundred-percent, Grade-A, executive manure." Tracy slugged back a good portion of her drink, craving the sweet comforting burn of the bourbon.

"I thought there was something not right about him." Cynthia nodded smugly. "When you genuinely come from nothing like Tracy and me, you recognize when it's being put on."

"Are you *sure?*" Missy shook her head in bewilderment. "I mean he was so—*nice.*"

"I thought he was a straight arrow, too." Allegra tilted her head, frowning. "I did think it was peculiar that he told all those stories to strangers, but I didn't sense he was lying. No irregularities whatsoever in his aura."

"He was lying. Through his perfect pearly whites." Tracy gulped down another healthy dose of her Manhattan.

"Well it's an amazing coincidence he showed up at the beach and then again...at your...oh." Missy looked pityingly at Tracy. "No coincidence, huh?"

"Not the slightest bit of one." Tracy tried to keep her tone light and sarcastic, but it came out sounding bitter and hurt instead. "He wanted to check us out."

"But surely he didn't expect you to invite him to the party. Why would he risk going if he was a fake?"

"Because it was the perfect opportunity to find out what kind of people we are so he could get a better shot at the account."

"It is a little strange, though, Tracy." Allegra tapped her finger on her cheek. "Why would he go on to try and seduce you, then accuse you of being a boy collector if he just wanted to know how to get your business?"

"So to speak." Cynthia waggled her eyebrows.

"Because he was sure a 'collector' like me would never recognize him dressed as a CEO. He could do whatever he wanted, play the role of the boy toy, maybe even get lucky. What fun that would have been! Score with the boss's daughter without her having any idea who you were."

"I can't believe that's all it was." Missy put a gentle hand on Tracy's arm. "That amazing connection between you—that wasn't just about getting lucky."

Tracy swallowed hard. "Who's to say whether he felt it that way?"

"Oh, he felt it all right." Cynthia nodded firmly. "You should have seen how he looked at you when you went outside onto the deck."

Tracy tried very hard to keep hold of the cauldron of boiling oil that Cynthia's words were fast turning into the massage variety. No question, when they'd met again at the 21st Century offices, the chemistry had still been there, potent as ever.

"Well, thank goodness you didn't sleep with him." Cynthia chuckled. "Even I would be glad I didn't in your situation."

"Oh, but you wouldn't have, Tracy...would you?" Missy bit her lip anxiously.

Tracy tipped back the last of her drink, a warm relaxing glow spreading through her body, making her feel reckless and confessional. "Actually, yes."

Missy gasped. Allegra nodded. Cynthia grinned. "Atta girl."

"I would have. I've never felt anything like that...need before. The problem is..." She stared down at her empty glass, euphoria making a quick exchange with sinking uncertainty. "The problem is..."

Cynthia tsk-tsked. "Uh-oh. You got it bad."

"What?" Missy looked from Cynthia to Tracy and back. "What do you mean?"

"She still wants to."

Missy's brows drew together. "Still wants to what?"

Tracy drew in a huge breath and let it out in a doomed sigh. "Sleep with him, Missy. I still want to sleep with him."

"Oh no!" Missy shook her head. "But you can't. Not after—"

"I know I can't. I didn't say I was going to. I just said I wanted to." Her face twisted, the alcohol bringing on an unusual overdose of self-pity. "But I also want to send him a crate of attack dogs. That's the trouble. That's the trouble with my whole life. I'm a walking, breathing conflict. I don't want to stay at 21st Century, but I don't want to leave. I don't *want* all this money, but I don't want to give it away." She furrowed her brow, feeling a little unsteady. "And I'm whining too much. I want to stop."

"I think you need food." Allegra took Tracy's elbow and steered her toward the hostess with Cynthia and Missy following. "Problems are always worse when your blood sugar is low and your electrolytes are out of balance."

"And when you come so close to finding someone so right, only to be disappointed."

"And when you haven't gotten any in *months*."

Ten minutes later, they were seated at a table in the noisy bustling dining area, the three women absorbed in the familiar menus, Tracy staring at hers without registering a single entrée. Finally she flung it to the table. "What's worse, Dad suddenly has all this experimenting to do and assigned me to work closely with Paul."

"Ugh." Cynthia folded her menu and shuddered. "Matchmaking at its most misguided."

"Wait until I tell him the first meeting is supposed to take place Tuesday evening at Paul's apartment."

"What?" The three women spoke at once.

"Something about it being more conducive to the easy flow of ideas." She quoted Paul and rolled her eyes. "Like a mental laxative."

"He's right." Allegra nodded vigorously. "It's been proven. A comfortable happy body equals a comfortable productive brain."

Cynthia snorted. "Sounds like a setup to me. Are you two the only lovebirds attending?"

"No, thank God. Two of his colleagues will be there."

"Oh, well that's okay, then." Missy sighed with relief. "Your dad won't mind."

"I take it you didn't tell your dad about Paul being Dan?" Cynthia asked. "He didn't figure it out?"

"No." Tracy made a sound of disgust. "He was so excited about Paul's work. The tomatoes were Mom's pet project and I think he wants the launch to be successful for her sake. At the same time, I can't stand *not* telling him. It's like lying."

"I think you should definitely tell him. Honesty is always best. Because sooner or later you get trapped in lies and misunderstandings," Missy said.

"I agree with Missy." Allegra folded her arms and pushed back her cascade of colored bracelets. "You start lying and your spirit gets all twisted up. Then you get indigestion, back pain, skin problems, you name it."

Cynthia leaned back and frowned thoughtfully. "Maybe you should tell him. Then Daddy can help you cook up some kind of horrible revenge—after Paul delivers on the ad campaign of course."

"I also think you should come clean to Paul about knowing who he is, Tracy. People do a lot of strange things for very good reasons. I don't know why he lied. You don't know. But he does. And you could give him a nice chance to tell you. Maybe the two of you could still work things out."

"What, are you *nuts?*" Cynthia stared at Missy in horror. "The guy's a total creep. He deserves public humiliation. He deserves figurative castration. He deserves to have his member exposed for the bite-size cocktail wienie it is."

"*Cynthia!*" Missy slumped in her seat and pointed surreptitiously to the just-arrived waitress, her cheeks flaming.

"Hello, ladies. Ready to order?"

The women ordered—Allegra went on and on with her list of substitutions and requests for organic produce; Cynthia let drop the chef's first name and ordered dishes not on the menu; Missy apologized for wanting something they were out of. Tracy ordered the first thing her eyes lit on because she didn't even care what she ate. Her mind was so busy sorting out the advice and the feelings that her stomach's needs were purely secondary.

Telling Paul she'd figured out his little game wasn't going to happen. If he wanted their association to be based on lies that was exactly what he'd get. After all, it wasn't as if they were heading for any kind of long-term relationship, romantic or otherwise. Certainly not as long as he kept up the pretense. The move toward honesty would have to come from him.

But she probably should tell her father about "Dan." No matter how talented Paul was, if he'd been dishonest in one thing, he could easily be dishonest in another aspect of his business. She owed it to her father so he could be on his guard, be careful. Whether or not he wanted to confront Paul with the knowledge was up to him. At least Tracy wouldn't feel she was holding anything back anymore. Now that she and her dad only had each other for family, that was all-important.

And seeing how talking the problem over with her friends had helped, how their concern and support shrank Paul/Dan down to a manageable size, having her dad in on the problem would give her another ally in the war for repossession of her sanity.

"Okay. I'll do it."

Three female heads whipped around. "What?"

"I'll tell my dad in a cool, reasonable way that Paul is a sneaking opportunistic jerk from hell." She lifted her water glass, feeling balance and control already returning. "First chance I get."

"SO YOU GOT a hot date tonight." Dave forked up a huge mouthful of kung pao chicken from the take-out carton he'd brought over to Paul's place.

Paul sent him a glare over his nearly untouched plate and re-restudied the 21st Century file he'd brought home with him. "It's not a date. Tracy is coming over to sit in on our usual company brainstorming session with Karen and Jim. It's work, Dave. She's a client. One I happen to want to make a good impression on for personal reasons. But not the ones you mean."

"So you're not nervous?"

"No."

Dave gestured at Paul's jiggling knee with his chopstick. "I see."

Paul relaxed his leg. "I always do that when I'm pumped for a session."

"Pumped?"

"Professionally speaking, yes."

"Oh, pro*fes*sionally pumped."

Paul rolled his eyes and turned a page over in the file. "Look. I admit, Tracy isn't quite the usual client. I was pretty angry over what happened last month. But that was last month. Now, I'm excited about what The Word can do for 21st Century and what 21st Century can do for me. If I can show Tracy along the way that all beach bums aren't what they seem, so much the better, but I'm not letting it get to me."

He turned another page, pleased with how rational he sounded. Maybe it wasn't entirely true that he wasn't angry anymore. But after seeing her in the office with her dad, after seeing what a good match their companies were, he'd realized that going for revenge was a pretty bad idea. As long as there was capitalism, there would be women like Tracy who valued money more than humanity. If he could change her mind even a little he'd have done some good, but he wasn't going to hold his breath. And he wasn't going to risk hijacking his own success by getting involved in destructive behavior.

As for his attraction, he was pretty sure that would soon be a thing of the past as well. You couldn't stay attracted to someone once you discovered aspects of their character that were distasteful to you. Maybe Dave could, but Paul couldn't. Granted, in the conference room at 21st Century, he and Tracy had still exchanged some powerful vibes, but Paul was pretty sure those were lingering in his head from their time on the beach. He'd be willing to bet that tonight, with the exciting job ahead of them and in the easy familiar company of Karen and Jim, his feelings for Tracy would be redefined into something easily manageable. Like polite deference to her as a client and casual indifference to her as a woman.

"Paul?"

Paul closed the folder and looked up impatiently. "What."

"Does the word *denial* mean anything to you?"

"Look, Dave. I know you have this idea that we're some kind of match, but please. Leave it. It's totally unrealistic. As long as she has this 'us and them' attitude, I can't handle any kind of real friendship with her. Especially considering where she came from. I can't respect anyone who thinks money makes a difference." Paul stood up and looked pointedly at his watch. "I have to get ready."

"Okay, okay." Dave gathered the remains of the Chinese food and pushed the cartons back into the plastic grocery bag. "I'm outta here. But I'm betting one nice intimate tête-à-tête talking about tomatoes is all it will take to show you I'm right. Very sexy vegetable, the tomato."

"Which is scientifically classified as a fruit. And two other people will be here, who have done this dozens of times before, which will make it tête-à-tête-à-tète-à-tête and not at all intimate."

"I wouldn't be too sure about that, Paul."

Something about his tone made Paul's head snap around. "Excuse me?"

"Your secretary is pretty cute, I ever tell you that?"

"No." Paul stared at him warily. "Why are you changing the subject?"

"She and I went out a few times."

"Susie? Geez-oh-man, is there *anyone* you missed?"

Dave strolled over and put his arm around Paul's shoulders in a mock-fatherly gesture. "The thing is, Paul. When The One comes along, you can't take chances, you can't play games. You gotta go for it."

Paul pushed him away and put his hands on his hips. He smelled a rat the size of a Usinger salami. "Elaborate, please."

"I'm guessing Tracy is *It* for you. Susie, she owes me one, so I cashed in by having her innocently pass along a couple of phone numbers." He reached the door and opened it. "And you're my friend so I always owe you one."

A very, very bad feeling began creeping up Paul's spine. He had to take a deep breath to make sure his voice would come out evenly. "What are you talking about, Dave?"

"Did I forget the point? I'm sorry. Karen and Jim can't make it tonight. They suddenly had other plans." Dave tilted his head to leave the apartment, then ducked back in and winked. "So tonight it's just you, Tracy...and her tomatoes."

Slam.

"Wha..." Paul stared at the closed door, his mind reeling. He lunged for it, then changed direction abruptly and hauled ass to the telephone, yanking his Palm Pilot V out of his pocket on the way. Richards.

Richards. There it was. He dialed, paced two steps and turned, two steps and turned, two steps and turned. No answer. She must have already left.

Karen. He speed-dialed her cell phone. *Ring... Ring... Ring...* Her voice mail picked up. *Damn.* Not answering. No point leaving a message. He needed someone here *now.*

Jim.

Ring... Ring—

"Hello?"

"*Jim.*" He raised his eyes and thanked the ceiling in a silent prayer of relief. "This is Paul. About tonight, I—"

"Oh, yeah. Thanks for cancelling. My kids are in a camp show tonight. They were bummed I wouldn't be there. When are we rescheduled for?"

"We're not. We're on tonight."

"What? But your friend said you had other—"

"I know. But...Tracy's already on her way. I'm here by myself. No one else is coming. We'll be—" Paul stopped pacing and squeezed his eyes shut. God, he sounded like a complete panicked mess. He was about to tell a colleague that he was freaking at the thought of being alone with a client. This was ludicrous. Tracy had no idea he was Dan, wouldn't at all be remembering that the last time they'd been together the emotional climate, if not the conversation, had revolved entirely around sex. Tracy was simply coming over to talk about her company's product. He was here to see that they could come up with some good ideas for selling it. Period. He was acting as if he were a teenage virgin introduced to Miss September and told he had ten minutes to give her multiple orgasms.

"Paul?"

"Yes, I'm here." He forced a smile into his voice. He was a professional. She was a professional. Together they would be thoroughly and completely...professional. End of story. He took a deep breath.

"Have a great time at your kids' show, Jim. Everything's under control."

5

TRACY SLAMMED DOWN the bedroom phone in her single woman house in Wauwatosa and sank onto the twin bed she'd bought secondhand after college. Her dad had gone up to the farm last weekend and must be spending his time in the greenhouse with his cell phone turned off. She'd been trying to reach him to tell him about Paul and Dan and how they had the remarkable quality of being the same person. Considering she was about to visit the lion's den—no, make that the weasel's lair—being able to expose Paul to her father and enjoy a little paternal outrage would have given her an extra boost of courage and moral fortitude.

At Paul's house she'd be totally out of her element, while he oozed around, completely at home in his. Even though Tracy was already painfully familiar with the feeling of being out of her element thanks to her new wealthy status, the prospect of this meeting still made her a little uneasy. A little nervous. And a little fluttery, darn it.

She scowled into the scarred dresser mirror. Worse, she'd had to come home to change because a nervous waitress dumped her lunch hamburger into her lap. No way was Tracy showing up at Perfect Paul's stained with ketchup and smelling of the deep fryer.

Which meant adios to the dull navy suit and high-necked blouse that had been so perfect for the occasion. Which meant going for her next most conservative outfit—the soft-rose suit Mom bought her several years ago, which was unfortunately quite becoming, though probably hopelessly out of style by now and a little too warm for the weather. Which meant Tracy was now furious at herself for being pleased that she looked nice all the way down to her underwear, because she'd changed that, too, at the last minute when the ratty old stuff she'd put on to feel defiantly unsexy started creeping into places it shouldn't.

This was torture.

The clock radio her dad gave her in high school made a grinding noise as the minute wheel revolved to change numbers. Six-forty-two. Time to leave. It would take a little over fifteen minutes to get from her house to Paul's lakeside condominium in Milwaukee.

Tracy closed her eyes, clenched her teeth and inhaled a hissing breath. She could do this. She *would* do this. Sail in with a show-me-the-money attitude and be gracious yet demanding, charming but relentlessly professional. After all, Tracy Richards was in the driver's seat. She was the boss, wielding the whip. He and his colleagues would be in boot-licking, butt-kissing, grovel mode.

She could do this.

Seventeen minutes later she stood outside Paul's apartment and grimly stabbed her finger on his buzzer. *Gracious and demanding. Charming and professional.* The door swung open and she braced herself against the flood of attraction she knew was coming.

It came. And how.

His face was slightly flushed, which made his blue eyes look even bluer and even more penetrating. His top button was undone, tie crooked, jacket hanging open, hair not quite perfect. He even looked a little guilty, as if she'd caught him in the middle of making violent love to someone's wife.

Entirely possible.

She quirked a condescending eyebrow the way Cynthia did so well, and smiled as coldly as she could manage with a primal furnace raging inside her. "Have I come at a bad time?"

"No, not at all. I was just..." He gestured her in. "Not at all. Come on in."

Tracy walked through the spacious foyer into the living room and quickly narrowed her eyes, which had been about to shoot wide open. The place looked like a page out of *Ostentatious Decorating for Very Very Rich People.* Glass and brass and iron and textured muted colors here, and modern eclectic art pieces there, and chairs and a table that looked like something out of the twenty-fourth century. Even though she knew squat about furniture and cared less, she could tell this place had been done professionally by someone instructed to get only the best of everything.

She stood there in her five-year-old suit, with scuffed decade-old shoes, and wished she'd worn her ratty underwear after all. Lord, what pretension. The place didn't even look like a *home* for heaven's sake. It looked like a museum exhibit. A very *empty* museum exhibit. She frowned. An empty museum exhibit with glass kidney-shaped Martian coffee table featuring a basket of 21st Century tomatoes, a bottle of wine and...two glasses. Where the hell were the other people from his company?

"I tried to call you."

"Oh?" She turned and met Paul's eyes, then looked away. If they were going to be working together she had to find some way to deal with this chemistry. But he stood in the room watching her, hands on his hips which seemed to broaden his already broad chest and emphasize the width of his nicely wide shoulders. And he had this speculative, sort of apprehensive look on his face, as if he was about to deliver bad news and cared what she thought, which, considering she was practically his employer, he better.

"I'm afraid it's going to be just you and me tonight." He put his hands in his pockets and bounced on his heels. "Karen and Jim can't make it."

This time she had no trouble looking at him, because she was trying to send killer laser beams out of her eyes that would get inside his brain and crunchy-fry it. "They can't make it."

"No. I'm sorry. I tried calling, but you must have already left." He crossed to the George Jetson coffee table and picked up the wine.

Pressure built behind Tracy's eyes until she thought she was going to shoot steam out the top of her head like a train. What kind of employees "couldn't make it" to a meeting with an important client? She'd suspect a sleazy come-on except even Paul wouldn't be stupid enough to put his company's reputation on the line with his biggest account to date. And by the way he fumbled with the wine and didn't meet her eyes, she could tell he was as embarrassed and uncomfortable as he bloody well ought to be.

"I have the supplies here." He ripped the foil off the bottle and pointed to a cassette recorder on the coffee table. "I already explained a little of how we do things. We can still get some good work done."

Tracy looked doubtfully at the unblemished cream-colored couch. Snuggled up together, sipping wine, discussing stream-of-consciousness tomatoes and fighting back attraction she couldn't put behind her as easily as he apparently could? No thanks.

"Why don't I come back another time when they can make it."

The instant the words were out of her mouth she wished them unsaid. One thing to be uncomfortable with the situation, yet determined to make the best of it. But by admitting her discomfort out loud, when he hadn't done anything overtly improper, she'd transformed the atmosphere from Tracy and Paul, colleagues at a meeting, to he-man and nervous she-woman, aware they were alone in a perfectly decorated apartment. That had a bedroom in it. With a bed.

Terrific.

He turned and looked at her. "Why?"

"I don't..." She blushed and was immediately even more furious with herself. She'd vowed to approach this as a purely professional venture, exactly as he was having no trouble doing. Instead she was freaking like a virgin catching her first glimpse of a penis.

"Look, Tracy. Karen and Jim got crossed signals. A...colleague needed them for something else tonight. It was a scheduling mistake for which I'm very embarrassed. Obviously this is not how I wanted our relation—our professional interaction to start. I know the wine and dim lights make it look suspicious. But this *is* how we work. It's extremely effective in allowing ideas to emerge freely. I hope you understand that I'm only interested in your toma—in promoting your company's tomatoes."

His voice rang with easy sincerity. Tracy nodded, trying not to think wistfully of that moment on the beach when it seemed his interest in her had nothing to do with her company's tomatoes and everything to do with her own admittedly meager ones. And trying harder not to feel rejected and disappointed seeing as how she suspected all along he no longer felt that way.

"Heavens." She bolstered her mouth into a carefree smile. "I was concerned we'd be wasting time without their input. That's all. This is fine."

"Oh." He stood clutching the wine, looking so mortified Tracy actually felt badly for lying to someone who was a pro at it. "Well, good. Have a seat. I'll pour the wine."

She sat. Stiffly at first, then leaned back on the admittedly comfortable sofa, determined not to look at all discomfited, and managed not to roll her eyes when he made a big show of smelling the cork, then swirling and tasting a small amount of wine in his glass before he poured out her portion. He definitely had moments of being human, but she couldn't forget the huge gulf of values that separated them. Keeping that in mind would give her the strength to get through the evening.

She accepted her glass and smiled calmly right into his killer blues without even spilling on herself at the now familiar charge of electricity through her body.

To her shock, he broke the eye contact first.

"So. What kind of music turns you on?—That is, what stimulates your—I mean what... Jazz okay?" He mumbled a few words under his breath that his mother would probably not have allowed, and waited for her response.

Tracy pulled her mouth shut before it could give into its desire to gape unattractively. The little part of her that felt disappointed and rejected when he verbalized his lack of interest so convincingly suddenly sat up straight and paid close attention. Maybe, just maybe, she wasn't the only one rattled here. Maybe that electricity had doubled back and charged him up as well.

A curious elation grew and spread inside her, along with the desire to find out for sure and the courage to do just that.

She nodded slowly, and sent him the most innocent sultry stare she could manage. "I've always found jazz very stimulating, Paul."

His mouth opened as if to speak, but no sound came out. He cleared his throat and walked over to a sound system that had more knobs and dials than a 747, stood in front of it and yanked at his tie knot with one finger.

Then he pushed both hands through his hair and mumbled something else she was too far away to catch.

Her elation grew and sparked into heated, dizzy breathlessness.

Oh. My. Goodness. He still wanted her.

The rousing strains of a jazz combo burst into the apartment. Paul turned and grinned, apparently back in balance, and played an accompanying passage on air piano. "Oscar Peterson. My hero."

Tracy nodded and took a sip of her wine. Then another. Then a nice tidy gulp. If they were on even ground, she could keep it together just fine. She, Tracy Richards, *femme unextraordinaire* could stay intact and feel pretty damn good about herself and her ability to cope under enemy fire. In the process they might even get some good work done for 21st Century Produce tomatoes.

"Now." He settled himself on the couch next to her, picked up his wine and took a long savoring sip. "We usually start by passing around the product or a picture, touching, smelling, or in this case tasting, to see what aspects are its strongest selling points, how it reaches us, what images it provokes. Okay? The only rule is that you do everything out loud. Even something that seems totally stupid can often lead to a great ad idea. No censoring. We usually write everything down, but since there are only two of us we'll use the recorder. You with me?"

"I'm with you."

"Comfortable?"

"Fine."

"Okay. Let's see..." He pressed the record button on the player, picked up a tomato and turned it over in his hands, leaned over it and furrowed his brow. "Juicy. Acid-sweet."

Tracy picked up another and swept her thumbs over the smooth skin, trying not to feel self-conscious. "Uh...red." She laughed nervously. "Seedless."

"That's fine." He reached over and laid his hand briefly on her arm. "Relax. Keep going."

She concentrated hard on the tomato, trying to ignore the still-touched feeling on her arm, trying to ignore the man altogether and give herself over to the task at hand. "Ripe. And round."

"Smooth." His voice dropped; he drew the word out, as if he were reciting seductive poetry. "Firm."

Oh. My. Goodness. She stared harder at the fruit, feeling the glow of wine take hold, making her cheeks flush and her body hum, suddenly aware of where this might lead them and not at all sure she didn't want to follow. "Luscious."

"Succulent...yielding."

Tracy took another gulp of wine. "Heavy. Ripe on the vine."

"Ripe." His voice deepened further, not overtly suggestive, but not entirely innocent either. "And ready."

Tracy's breathing turned shallow; she kept her eyes fixed on the tomato in her hand, aware of him, of the dangerous flirtation, of the way it made her feel warm and alive and warm and...very warm. "Alive. And warm. Scented of the earth."

"The hot smell of summer."

"Like red ripe balls."

"Like globes."

"Full of flavor." She was whispering now; the darkness and music and his nearness charged the room with eroticism.

"Bite it."

She licked her lips nervously, leaned back against the sofa cushion, unbuttoned the single button of her jacket, the enticing rush of adrenaline daring her to go further. "Peel it, then bite."

"Slip off the skin."

"Peels like a dream."

"Naked now."

"Free."

"Beautiful." His voice clouded into a husky murmur. "Tempting."

Tracy let out a gasping breath. A drum solo pounded hot rhythms into the air around them. She should stop this; she really should stop this. But it was so damn exciting.

She closed her eyes, unable to resist. "Taste it."

"It's dripping."

"Lick the juice."

"So sweet."

"I want more."

"So do I, Tracy."

Her eyes shot open at his urgent whisper. He wasn't staring at his tomato anymore. And the hunger in his eyes didn't look as if it would be sated by produce.

Tracy pushed herself forward to sit upright. This

was crazy. Insane. She'd never done anything like this in her life, never even been tempted. The game was about to move beyond flirtation and she wasn't ready. What the hell was the matter with her? She'd invited more than she planned to go through with and she detested women who did that. No way could she start anything with this man. There were about a million reasons *not* to and only one *to*. And that one was pretty hot and pulsing and powerful at the moment, even worse than when they'd been out on the beach together.

Damn. Why wasn't she wanton and proud of it like Cynthia? Why couldn't she dive into this right now and wake up tomorrow with most of it already forgotten? But not her. She'd fall madly in love with him even though he was the world's biggest jerk, then she'd follow him around like a smitten puppy until he had to kick her repeatedly to get rid of her.

Been there, lived that. Time for the cooldown. Even this lust wasn't strong enough to override the painful bite of reality and self-knowledge.

"I think maybe that's enough."

He leaned away from her and took a long breath as if he was bringing himself back from somewhere else, then clicked off the tape player and hit another button to rewind it. "Yes. Okay. I think you're right."

"You'd better erase that. Now." She gestured to the tape. Once that was destroyed, their conversation never happened.

He nodded, pressed Stop, then Record again, and shoved the machine under the sofa cushion next to him to muffle the incoming sound and effectively erase the tape. "We'll get Karen and Jim in on it and try again."

"Yes. Okay." She got to her feet at the same time he did, Oscar Peterson swinging out a mellow tune now as if he were playing the accompanying score to their evening. They faced each other in the dim light and she caught her breath. No question, Paul Sanders was gorgeous. His blue-gray eyes practically glowed in this light.

"Tracy."

"Yes." She folded her arms across her chest.

"Are we going to ignore what happened?"

She bent her head and studied his fancy finished floor. "I think ignoring it is a good idea."

"Why?"

"Because you're working for my father. And essentially for me." She swept her arm in a circle, indicating his apartment. "And we're totally different."

He glanced around him. "What, you think I'm the sum total of my decor?"

"Maybe not. But I think home says a lot about a person."

"Oh, really?" He put his hands in his pockets and set himself in a deliberately casual stance that didn't hide the challenge. "What does mine say about me?"

"Money is important to you. Status. Showing the world you're one of the ones who made it."

"I see. What's your place like?"

"I have old stuff. Worn-out, secondhand stuff." She pictured her kitchen: the flowery curtains Mom made shortly after she and Dad were married; canisters with strawberries on them from the fifties... Her bedroom with the rocker brought up from the farmhouse... "Stuff I've owned all my life that has a lot of meaning to me."

He narrowed his eyes. "Oh, okay, so I'm shallow and pretentious and you have the depth of the ages, is that it?"

She winced. It *had* come out a little like that. "I'm sorry. I'm just describing what I see."

"I'll tell you what, Tracy." He took a step closer which made her hug her arms tighter around herself. "I'll come over to your place sometime and tell you what I think of you."

Tracy took in a deep breath. She deserved that. He hadn't said the words angrily necessarily, but that hard edge emerged from his tone as it had the night on the beach when he accused her of wanting him for casual sex. A tone at odds with the soft pampered Luxury Boy image.

"I guess it's only fair you get a shot at me."

His mouth widened into a slow sexy grin. "Maybe I'd better leave that one alone."

Tracy laughed and felt herself blushing. She could spot BS a mile away, and she'd certainly detected bushels of it in Paul. But in moments like these when they connected, even from opposite sides, it was hard to know what to think. Hard to figure out who he really was. The man kept jumping in and out of the tidy little labelled box she wanted him to stay in so she could feel nothing but contempt. Because he was sort of charming and funny at times. And of course *People* magazine hadn't ever seen him or he'd be on the cover of their "Sexiest Man Alive" issue for all eternity.

But then there was that other side that told the lies and cared too much what others thought; the side that worshipped wealth and status, all things utterly repulsive to her.

"Where did you grow up?"

He looked surprised at her sudden question, then eyed her warily, both of which she expected. Obviously he couldn't repeat the tearjerker "Dan" spread around at her dad's party. This time he'd have to tell the truth.

"Why do you ask?"

"Because I want to know."

"Fair enough." He narrowed his eyes, glanced at the floor, the wall to his right, then looked evenly into her face. "I was born…in Concord, Massachusetts, my parents were doctors, I had a succession of nannies and private tutors until I was old enough to go to Exeter Academy and then Harvard. From there I built my own business with capital invested by my father. I was born with a silver spoon and turned it to gold. Now with your company I'm hoping to go platinum. Does that answer your question?"

"Yes." She wove her fingers together and stared down at them. "It does."

Except it didn't at all. He was lying. Instinctively she knew. There was nothing but polite detachment in his voice. None of the repressed pain, the bitterness, the curt wrenching of bare facts from his lips as there'd been on the beach when he talked to her about his childhood of poverty. Missy and Allegra had both sensed his sincerity at the party, under the "poor-me" delivery. That was the real story after all.

Her lip curled in disgust. How typical. Even if he couldn't repeat the details he'd already used, he could just as easily have invented a story closer to the truth. But in his new guise as Paul the WonderAchiever, he couldn't admit to having been "one of them," even knowing Tracy grew up the same way he had. Some people would be proud to have come so far on their own. To have gotten that silver or gold or platinum spoon after they'd been born sucking fast-food plastic. But not Mr. Appearances R Us.

A miserable weight dragged down her shoulders, pulled on her heart, settled somewhere around her toes. Okay, so she was disappointed. She still couldn't handle the fact that she was so attracted to him and he wasn't the kind of person she could respect. Maybe because that kind of split had simply never happened to her. She'd like to think she had some kind of sense when it came to picking out a partner. That over the years humans might have evolved past simple chemical attraction to mix in some other factors appropriate to mating for the long term.

Apparently not.

"How about you?"

"I'm sorry?" She shoved herself out of her thoughts and registered his look of polite curiosity.

"Where did you grow up?"

He probably already knew. "I grew up in Northwestern Wisconsin, a little town called Oak Ridge. Really a conglomeration of farms. We didn't have much, but the land was beautiful and it fed us body and soul if you'll pardon me waxing poetic about it. Then my dad's experiments started bearing fruit, so to speak, and now..." she shrugged. "You know the rest."

"Interesting."

She blinked up at him. "What?"

"Your face."

"What is so interesting about my face?"

"Many things." He gestured to the sofa. "Do you want to sit back down?"

Tracy turned and contemplated the sofa. Sitting back down with him meant committing to a talk of some minutes before she could politely get away. Standing here was safer, because she could press the eject button the second it all got too much.

"I don't think...I mean—"

"Okay." He held up his hands in surrender, watching her intently. "We can stand if it feels safer."

Tracy bristled. "I don't feel unsafe."

He put his hands down, still making her feel he was registering every tiny shift of her mood. "If you say so."

"I should go." She didn't move, even though she told her legs to get walking immediately to the exit. Apparently she was more of an adrenaline junkie than she thought, because even after she'd just received more unflattering data for her mental file on him, being here was a rush like nothing she'd ever felt.

"You can't go yet." The quiet statement gave her a

little thrill of being wanted. Even if all he wanted was conversation. "I still haven't told you about your face."

She laughed. "How could I live through the night without knowing what you thought of my face?"

"Exactly. When you were talking about growing up..." He took off his jacket and flung it across the room to land neatly on the sofa, then loosened his tie. "Do you mind?"

Tracy gulped for air. Nothing was calculated or deliberately seductive about his movements, but his natural grace and the magnificent body under his clothes made it impossible not to fantasize about his shirt following, and his pants and...so on. "No problem."

"Anyway." His tie went spinning after the jacket. "Where was I?"

You were just carrying me into the bedroom for an all-night sexathon. "You were starting this evening's episode of 'All About Tracy's Face.'"

He chuckled as if she absolutely delighted him, which made her blush tally for the evening exceed all previous records. "When you were talking about your life on the farm, your face went dreamy and romantic."

"Oh?" She mentally checked her features to make sure there was no lingering trace of dreamy and romantic. Or worse, hot and bothered after what she'd just been thinking.

"Then when you started talking about your father's success..." He shrugged.

"Let me guess." Tracy wrinkled her nose. "Complete lack of dreamy and romantic?"

"Yeah." He nodded. "What's that about?"

She looked around pointedly at his gussied-up decor, then fixed him with an are-you-kidding? stare that lacked any bite. "Nothing you'd understand."

"Oh, of course not." He whacked his forehead in a what-was-I-thinking? gesture. "Me, the great Capitalist Pig, contaminated by the filthy luxury coating my sty."

She couldn't suppress a grin. "That's right."

"And you the noble lover of earth, letting it get you all dirty and uncomfortable...but in a pure and honest way."

"I was happy growing up on the farm." Her voice caught. She pressed her lips together.

"Ergo you're not happy now." He took another step closer. "Why not, Tracy?"

She moved toward the door. He was too close. This conversation was too close. Everything was too damn close. She should be sharing her problems with people she loved and trusted, like the girls, like her father. Not this man, this inscrutable combination of sincerity and artifice, who made her want to jump his body and donate it to science at the same time. "I'd better go."

He made a sound of impatience. "You, Tracy Richards, are a giant clucking chicken."

"Why?" She scowled at him. "Because I won't share my inner thoughts with someone I just met and have no reason to trust?"

He looked startled for a second, then laughed and shook his head. "I'm sorry. You're absolutely right. Forgive me."

She nodded, taken aback by his retreat. "I still should go."

"I'd like you to stay."

"I don't think it's appropriate."

His eyebrows shot up. "Not appropriate to talk to me?"

Tracy fidgeted. "Not appropriate in the evening hours at your apartment."

"After what happened between us."

She fixed her gaze firmly on the third button of his shirt. "I guess."

"That's not what I want from you. It's...a factor, definitely. I won't pretend I'm not attracted to you. I am. But I was attracted to my teacher in kindergarten, and to my married neighbor in Massachusetts and to a cashier at my grocery store. They are all still alive and well and unmolested by me in any way."

She laughed. It was tempting. To give in, sit on the couch and sip wine and gradually drown herself in those eyes and in the seductive excitement of being with him. To see which side of him would dominate, which side would win. Whether he'd admit to his lies or tell new ones. And over it all was the thrill of knowing he wanted her and she wanted him.

But then what? After she left his persuasive presence, once she escaped from the tantalizing glimpses of someone she could enjoy, she'd be flattened by the reality of the total picture that was Paul Sanders. Once it came fully back home to her who he was and what he wanted in life, she'd wish she'd stayed stronger, resisted. Not given him more power, not allowed him to see anything of her without some guarantee that she'd see anything honest from him in return.

She smiled and primly buttoned her jacket. "I'll call you tomorrow. We can round up your colleagues and meet again later in the week."

He studied her until she bit her lip and walked to his front door.

"Sounds good." His voice behind her was brisk and businesslike. "If I'm not in when you call, my secretary will make the appointment."

He overtook her, reached around and opened the door. "Good night, Tracy."

"Good night."

She walked out of his apartment without meeting his eyes, half-wishing she was the kind of woman who could stay, knowing she'd spend the rest of the night alone in bed wondering what would have happened if she had.

6

PAUL CLOSED the door behind Tracy and leaned his head against it. What the hell just happened to him? She was a *client* for God's sake. Not just a client, *the* client. The one who would make his fortune, give him the security he craved, the final irrevocable sense that he had landed and wouldn't be heading back out any time soon.

How had he allowed that sexual tone to creep into what was supposed to be a professional exchange? All his good intentions, all his vows to keep his libido under control, all his assertions that his attraction was shallow and already half-passed had exploded in a rush of heated blood. At the sound of her voice. Describing tomatoes.

He turned to look guiltily at his Le Vele sofa and sighed. Those words. Her voice. That heated rush.

The tape player.

He crossed the room, dug it out from under the cushions and hit rewind. He'd done a ba-a-ad thing when she insisted he erase the tape. Pressed fast forward instead of rewind so the tape he made such a show of erasing was already blank.

And their brainstorming session was still intact.

The motor sped up for the last few seconds of the rewind, then stopped with a jerk. Paul took up his glass, emptied half the wine down his throat and set it carefully on his Tivoli coffee table. He sat down on the couch and stared at the tape inside the machine, at the brown shiny coil neatly wound on one side.

Then pressed play and leaned back.

Juicy. Acid-sweet.

He closed his eyes, pictured her next to him, earnestly staring at her tomato, her mouth bunched in concentration, forehead furrowed.

Ripe. And round.

He'd been glancing at her regularly by then, wondering if she knew what was happening, if she had any awareness of what the words were starting to signify.

Peel it, then bite.

Paul moved up off the sofa and back down; he was getting hard again, the way he had when he'd noticed her mouth relaxing, her brow smoothing, her skin glowing rosy pink. Then she'd leaned back on the couch, closed her eyes and he'd practically lost it.

Taste it.

He groaned and pushed his hips up against the straining fabric of his pants. She'd been incredible, drawn into passion by mere words. What would she do if he touched her? Kissed her? Tasted her?

I want more.

"So do I, Tracy." He whispered the words along with the tape and gave a short laugh that half-sounded like dismay. This was crazy. This was nuts. He'd go completely out of his mind before—

His door flew open. He grabbed the tape player and settled it in his lap. "For God's sake, Dave, can't you even knock?"

"You want to keep me out? Try locking your door."

"I lock it when I go to bed."

"So you haven't been there yet, eh? I heard her leave. Thought I'd give you a few minutes to compose your self." Dave glanced down at the tape player. "Apparently not enough minutes. Or are you into machinery now?"

Paul tossed the player aside in disgust. "Give me a break."

Dave sank next to him on the couch and crossed his huge feet on the coffee table. "Uh-oh, Paul The Grouch Man. Things didn't go so good?"

"What did you expect? You trick me into having her alone here when we're supposed to be colleagues. I'm lucky she didn't sue me for sexual harassment."

"Oh?" Dave sat up and took his feet off the table. "You harassed her sexually?"

"Of course not. We did some brainstorming for her toma—her *company's* tomatoes." He held his hand up to ward off Dave's inevitable bad joke. "Then she insulted my apartment and left. That's it."

Dave frowned. "She insulted your apartment?"

"Yes." Paul gathered up the wineglasses and the half-empty bottle. "She thinks I'm shallow and pretentious."

"Oh yeah? Well, she's only half-right." Dave followed Paul into the kitchen and settled his huge frame on a hand-painted wooden counter stool.

Paul glared at him. "Which half?"

"Pretentious."

"I like what my money can buy. There's nothing wrong with a genuine taste for the good stuff. Whoever said that poverty was noble wasn't poor. I know poverty. I did poverty. It sucks. Period."

"Okay, okay, man." Dave held up his hands. "I'm sorry, I really am. I can't even pretend to know what it's like, so I should just shut the heck up about it."

Paul allowed a grin on his face. "Yeah, you should."

Dave grabbed an apple from the bottom tier of a trio of hanging copper baskets and shined it on his shirt. "I'd say she really got to you. Am I right?"

Paul put the glasses in the dishwasher and mumbled out a "No."

"What?" Dave shouted thickly over a huge mouthful of apple. "What did you say?"

"I said, 'No,'" Paul shouted back. Maybe he was being childish not wanting to admit to Tracy's effect on him. But he knew what would happen if he did. Dave would start in with jokes about Tracy's tomatoes and how he could manage to get his hands on them. Jokes that would end sometime in the next millennium.

Right now he had to focus on the fact that he was working for her and her father. After he launched the 21st Century Produce tomatoes campaign and his and Tracy's professional relationship had solidified, then maybe he could take some time to find out what was between them. To start, he could confess about the Dan impersonation, which, given what he was discovering about Tracy, was turning out to have been a stupid, unnecessary mistake.

In the meantime, for the sake of his career, as far as Dave was concerned, and as far as Paul could fool himself into believing, he and Tracy were nothing more than colleagues.

"Right. No effect." Dave opened a corner cabinet and dropped the apple core in the trash. "So what are you going to do about this totally unaffecting woman who makes you hump tape recorders?"

"Dave..."

"Okay, I'm sorry. But seriously. She's got the wrong picture of you, obviously. You do have a fondness for the trend *du jour* in your decorating, but you're not shallow. Doesn't she know how you grew up?"

"No."

"So tell her."

"I can't."

"Why?"

"Because tonight I told her the complete opposite."

"Huh?" Dave's features twisted into disbelief. "You told her you grew up rich? Why the hell did you do that?"

Paul sighed and sealed the wine with a vacuum pump designed to keep spoiling oxygen out of the bottle. "I was angry at her assumptions about me, so I told her what she already thought, what she wanted to hear. It doesn't matter."

"Oh, right. Right." Dave nodded. "It doesn't matter. Because she means nothing to you."

Paul looked him right in the eye with a challenging stare. "That's right."

"Hmm." Dave's eyes narrowed speculatively then widened to their natural state. "Okay, I gotta go."

Paul grabbed his arm and stopped him leaving the kitchen. "What?"

Dave blinked innocently. "What, what?"

"That idea you just had. What is it?"

"What are you talking about?"

"Dave." Paul tightened his hold on Dave's huge arm

until the bigger man winced. "I think you've done enough."

"Sure, buddy. No problem. I'll leave it to you now." He winked and left the kitchen.

Paul heard his door closing and rolled his eyes. He had a bad feeling about this. He'd have to have another talk with Dave about his well-intentioned meddling. Maybe when he was a little cooler, and able to talk about Tracy without giving too much away.

He followed Dave's path to the front door and locked it securely. Turning, he surveyed his apartment, hands on his hips, trying to see it through her judgmental eyes.

The place was a masterpiece of taste and design. He'd hired the best decorating firm in Milwaukee and they'd been worth every penny. She acted as if he'd done something dirty.

He shrugged and walked into his bedroom, unbuttoning his shirt. She was strange about money, loaded in a way most of the world only dreamed about, yet wearing that old suit and scuffed shoes. As if she wouldn't allow herself to enjoy what she had, as if she wouldn't let herself adjust to what she'd become.

He shook his head. What a waste. He'd love to deck her out in finery. See those perfect legs peeking out from some skimpy designer creation. Show her what fun it could be to fly the Concorde and have dinner in Paris just for the hell of it. Simply because you *could*, damn it.

She had all that money, she should be taking part in what her new life could offer. To spit on the kind of opportunity so few people had was a crying shame. Worse, it was obstinate. She was living in a state of denial, refusing herself what she could have out of her one shot at living. For Paul, it was one of the worst sins imaginable.

His shirt missed the hamper on his first toss. He bent to retrieve it and stuffed it neatly inside. Maybe he could help her. Maybe he could introduce her bit by bit to some of the wonderful things money could buy. Let her find out firsthand, help her let go and let loose, enjoy the gift she had. Maybe invite her father along to make sure their attraction stayed on the back burner this time, where it belonged.

A slow grin spread over his face. He rushed to the phone and dialed.

"Hello, Chez Mathilde Restaurant."

"Hello. I'd like to make a lunch reservation for three. Day after tomorrow."

"DAD?" TRACY KNOCKED on his half-open office door and poked her head in, still carrying her briefcase and purse. She'd come straight here this morning, determined to have that little talk about Paul/Dan. Especially after last night. She badly needed someone to help get her grounded and see the man as he really was. She'd tried all night and all she'd gotten for her efforts were profoundly erotic dreams that had her reaching for her own release in the middle of the night.

Her father looked up from the stack of reports he was studying, smiled and gestured to the upholstered chair in front of his desk. "Hey, Tracy, come on in. Nice to see you, how was your weekend?"

"Okay. How was the farm?" Tracy plopped into the chair and blew a kiss at her father.

"Its usual beloved near-wreck of a self. I got some

good work done." He grimaced. "At least I figured out some things that won't work. Which always brings me closer to the final solution."

Tracy grinned. "Ever the optimist. I tried to call you about a million times."

"Did you? I'm sorry. I camped out in the greenhouse, turned off the phone. You know how I am when I work."

Tracy nodded and stared down at her fingers. Okay. It was time. She was going to tell him. One, two, three, okay...go.

...Okay, go.

Okay...

She gave a silent groan. This was horrible. Worse than horrible. She'd worried about telling her dad before because he might be disappointed and hurt to discover the deception. Because Paul was so right for 21st Century Produce tomatoes and she worried about jeopardizing that promising new relationship. Good reasons. But not good enough.

Now these not-good-enough reasons were complicated by a growing sense of...connection to Paul/Dan. Some weird feeling that she should talk to *him*, get his side first. Which was ridiculous. She certainly didn't owe him more loyalty than she owed her father. But still...

Her father cleared his throat. "So, uh, how was the meeting with Paul?"

"Good. Good." She felt herself blushing and wanted to growl with frustration. Dad wouldn't miss that little sign of discomfort.

She looked up from her twisting fingers to find him staring expectantly.

"Yes, Tracy?"

"It's about Paul."

His eyebrows shot up. *"Yes?"*

She glared at him. "Not like *that.*"

"Oh." His face fell, much to her disgust. "Then what? Out with it. I have ridiculous amounts of paperwork, which is even more revolting after having spent the weekend in peace on the farm."

She leaned forward eagerly. He'd never admitted that before. "Do you miss being there, Dad?"

"You're changing the subject."

"I want to know."

"Yes. I do. And whenever I miss being there, I go. Now what's this about Paul?"

"I mean do you miss living there, miss our old life?"

"Which part? Working my fingers to the bone or staying up all night worrying I wouldn't be able to feed you, let alone send you to college?"

Tracy shook her head. "We were happy there."

"Yes." He nodded seriously. "Yes, we were. And very uncomfortable and always near panic that it was going to come crashing down on us. Figuratively, I mean."

"Are you that happy now?"

He gave a small sad smile that sent pain into her heart. "No. I am not that happy now. But it's not the farm I miss. It's your mom. Now what's the deal with Paul?"

Tracy reached out and put her hands on her dad's forearms, resting on the desk, squeezing hard to show her love. "Okay. Do you remember last month, that guy who crashed our party at the beach?"

"Dan." He looked at her warily. "What about him?"

"Dan and Paul are the same person." She watched his face anxiously, knowing it would take a while for the full impact of the statement to hit and terrified she'd made the wrong decision in telling him.

He chuckled without humor. "I wondered when you'd figure that out."

Tracy's face froze into a wide-eyed, openmouthed stare.

Her dad chuckled again, this time, somewhat irritatingly, with plenty of humor. "Yes, I knew. Not terribly hard to put it together. Not even sure why he thought we wouldn't recognize him. Something about his clothes and attitude, probably."

"But...but..." Tracy leaned back in her chair and sent her mouth severe instructions to function properly. "It's disgusting."

"What is?"

"Everything. That he came to the party in the first place, knowing who we were..."

"Smart move to check out your target before you make your pitch. And we invited him in, don't forget."

"That he made such a point of how disadvantaged he was compared to the rest of us when it wasn't true..."

"Good disguise, seems to me."

"That he thought we were so shallow and pretentious that when he changed suits we wouldn't even recognize him..."

"Tracy." Her father stood, walked around the desk and sat on it next to her chair. "You didn't think I recognized him. Do you think I'm shallow and pretentious?"

"No, of course not. I thought...I thought..." She

pummeled her brain to get it to think what she had thought.

"You thought it was just a good disguise and I hadn't seen through it."

Tracy wrinkled her nose. "I guess."

Her father shrugged and drew her to her feet. "So did he."

"But—"

"Tracy, my love, I have ridiculous amounts of work to do. All I will say to you right now is that you are hell-bent on making him out to be the worst villain this side of Darth Vader, and you could do worse than taking some time to figure out why it's so important that he's loathsome."

He pulled her toward the door. Tracy followed dumbly, shaking her head. No matter how old you got, your parents couldn't stop totally missing the point of what you were trying to say. "The thing is, Dad, if he lied back then, he could lie again now."

"Sure he could." He leaned down and kissed the tip of her nose. "He could also burst in and take us out with a hand grenade, but I'm not going to start building bunkers in my office any time soon."

"Dad—"

He pushed her gently out the door. "And while you're figuring out why you so desperately need to dislike and distrust him, you might want to throw in a few thoughts on why you blush every time his name is mentioned."

He winked and closed the door, leaving her staring at the dark wood in total frustration. He'd done it again. Railroaded over her concerns with his own agenda. She had to admire him for it, even as she wanted to throw a tantrum on his fancy carpeted floor. Legions of professionals had left this office with the same dazed expression that was probably on her face right now—going in with one idea fixed firmly in their minds and leaving with whatever idea had been in his. It made him a damn good businessman, and a thoroughly irritating father.

She wasn't trying to make Paul out to be a monster, Paul was doing just fine by himself. And as for blushing, well, it was just a teeny bit embarrassing to be talking to her father about a business colleague to whom she'd said, "Lick the juice" the night before, without meaning tomatoes.

Tracy gave a sigh of resignation. The battle was over, the war still to be won. She'd try again later.

She headed into her office. Mia hung up the phone in a big hurry and turned to her computer which, judging by the screensaver, hadn't been touched in at least fifteen minutes.

"Oh, hi, Tracy. I'm almost done with the Graham letter. I'll have it on your desk in a sec. Here's your coffee."

"You don't have to get me coffee, Mia." Tracy picked up the Starbucks cup and took an appreciative sip.

Mia rolled her eyes. "You say that every morning. 'I don't mind. I was getting some for myself anyway,' which is what I say back to you every morning."

Tracy laughed and took another sip. "How was your date last night? This was Fred?"

"Frank. And it was okay." Mia shrugged and waved her red-polish-tipped fingers. "He's nice. But he's not Mr. Right."

"You always say that."

"Because I always know."

"How?" Tracy cleared her throat and adjusted her voice downward in case Mia got the wrong idea and thought Tracy was interested for some specific reason.

Mia stopped pretending to type and pushed back from the keyboard so her chair swiveled around to face Tracy. "When I meet Mr. Right, I'll know. All I'll have to do is look into his eyes and it'll be there. I'm telling you, when that happens, no matter where I am, I'm going to jump right into his arms and say, 'Yes, I'll marry you.'"

Tracy nearly spit a sip of coffee back into her cup. "What if he doesn't ask you?"

Mia gave a sigh of absolute romantic bliss. "Oh, he will."

"What if he's already married?"

"No." Mia shook her head emphatically. "He won't be. Because he's waiting for me, same way I'm waiting for him. It's only a matter of time."

"What if..." Tracy cleared her throat and made sure she was acting extremely nonchalant about the entire business. "What if he's not someone you end up liking? What if, for example, his values are totally different from yours?"

Mia looked at her as if Tracy needed prompt medical attention. "That would *never* happen. There are only three things you need to know. One, you look into his eyes the first time and it's right there."

"Right there?"

"Yeah." Mia tipped her blond head back and smiled dreamily at the ceiling. "Turns your insides out, makes you think lightning just struck."

Tracy banished the image of her first meeting with Paul on the beach and rolled her eyes. "Two?"

"Two, you can't stop thinking about him after you meet."

Tracy swallowed, then busied herself picking lint off her suit. "Three?"

"Three is the clincher." Mia leaned forward and looked carefully around. "You do things you never knew you wanted to do until you met him. It's like you discovered an entire part of yourself that was missing."

Tracy froze with her hand dangling a thread over Mia's wastebasket. "How do you know all this when you haven't ever experienced it yourself?"

"I know. Trust me. That's how it happens. And when it does, you better not turn your back, because that's your only chance at true love."

Tracy suppressed a snort. "Enough. I'm outta here. Give me the Graham letter when it's done."

She picked up her mail and went into her office. What the hell had possessed her to ask those kinds of questions? Obviously she wasn't going to get answers from Little Fanny Fairy Tale that had any relation to actual fact. Discussing research on the Manhunter theory would have to be saved for when Tracy and the girls had their next dinner.

She sat at her desk and put her purse in a lower drawer, grabbed a few papers from her in-box and stared at them. Shipping orders. She needed to look them over and sign.

Six lines into looking over, the papers slid from her hands.

Only chance at true love. Ha! Honestly. If Mia thought

her life was going to be all roses and romance she'd better think again. Boy, Tracy would like to bump into her in ten years. She'd be surrounded by piles of laundry and screaming children, her husband already on his fourth or fifth "true love" after her.

Ludicrous. To think you could build an entire life based on a moment's attraction.

Crazy. Tracy would get the Manhunters started on the road to reason, because although it was certainly possible she and Paul could put in some damn good time between the sheets, he was hardly her happily ever after. Just because some dreamer secretary believed in love at first sight meant absolutely nothing. Tracy was a solid, dependable, feet-on-the-ground kind of chick, and she wasn't going to let hormones or chemistry upset who she was and what she wanted in her life, whatever the hell that turned out to be.

So there.

She signed the orders and put them into another pile, drew out the next two papers and scanned them briefly.

Her phone rang, jolting her into instant awareness. She tried to squelch it; it wasn't him. Last night she said *she* would call. *He* wasn't going to. It wasn't him. So she could just calm the hell down and put the guy out of her mind where he seemed to have taken up permanent residence.

She picked up the receiver and spoke firmly into it.

"Tracy?" His deep voice sent lightning skittering through her body. She knew suddenly and without the slightest doubt that whatever he was going ask, she was going to do. Because last night, next to him in the dim light, flushed by wine and desire, she'd spouted erotic tomato-inspired poetry, which she never knew she'd wanted to do until she met him. And it had been like finding an entire part of herself that was missing.

She was doomed.

7

"READY TO GO TO LUNCH?" Tracy stuck her head into her dad's office and smiled way too brightly, which he would undoubtedly notice and put into his mental Tracy-loves-Paul file. So be it. He'd figure out the truth in time. Right now, all she could say was thank goodness Dad had been invited to this meal. Bad enough she had to sit with Paul at some fancy restaurant, trying to be professional, discussing tomatoes *again* when all either of them would be able to think about was the last time they'd tried it. If she had to be alone with him, she'd freak completely.

Her father covered the mouthpiece on his phone. "I'm sorry, you'll have to go without me."

Tracy freaked completely. *"What?"*

He glanced up at her shriek and raised his eyebrows. "Shipment of 21st Century pitless avocados got held up, and Guajolote, Texas needs them for a guacamole festival. I'm trying to reroute some from our Mexican growers. I can't leave."

"Dad?" Tracy tried to sound like a calm person and failed. If this was her father's idea of Matchmaking 301, he wasn't getting away with it. "Why haven't I heard anything about this guacamole festival before?"

"Si, senor. That's right." He covered the mouthpiece

again and held up a single sheet of fax paper. "Here. Have a good time."

Tracy marched over to him and took the paper. It was a photocopy of a newspaper article from some dinky cowtown bemoaning the terrible tragedy that might befall them if their precious avocados didn't arrive in time.

Except she'd never heard of Guajolote, and the layout of the article looked slightly strange. "Dad?"

He shook his head at her. "*Si. Si.*"

She reached over and grabbed the phone. "Who is this really?"

A torrent of Spanish came over a crackly long-distance line.

"Uh...sorry." Tracy swallowed and handed the phone back to her father. "Dad, why don't we reschedule the lunch to when—"

Her father's brows drew together, indicating a paternal storm on the way. "Go, Tracy. This meeting with Paul is important. We have to get this product launched ASAP."

She opened her mouth to protest and stopped herself. The more fuss she made the more suspicious he'd get and the more teasing and prying she'd have to endure. She squared her shoulders, saluted sarcastically and about-face-marched out his door. *Fine. Terrific.* Shoved into certain misery by guacamole.

Just for good measure, she stopped at her father's secretary's desk. "Becky?"

The older woman turned from her computer, beaming. "Yes, Tracy."

"Has my dad been working on anything special recently? I couldn't really talk to him. He was on the phone."

"Besides that horrible California holdup? Nope. He's under terrible strain. Those Texans have been calling every other hour, screaming for their avocados."

Tracy narrowed her eyes; Becky's clear blue gaze held steady, betraying nothing but utter sincerity.

"Okay, thanks." Tracy smiled and headed for the elevator, waiting until Becky couldn't see her to begin gnashing her teeth. The wailing, pulling of hair and head-banging would have to happen in the elevator, provided it was empty.

It wasn't. And by the time she reached the ground floor and made it to her car, most of the stages of total outrage and fury had passed her by and she was able to think logically and clearly as a mature adult.

Maybe she could be overcome by some horrible food allergy one bite into their lunch.

Maybe she could pretend she'd gotten into a car accident on the way over.

Maybe she could get Mia to call her away from lunch for something terribly urgent.

She drove up Kilbourn Avenue, knowing she wouldn't do any of those things, but enjoying the images anyway. One thing was certain, if she needed to, it would be easy to act sick. Her stomach was already in turmoil. She felt so dorky and out of place in fussy restaurants.

The hovering waiters reciting specials made from

things she didn't even know existed; the endless array of silverware suggesting she'd contaminate her fork beyond hope of reuse the second she touched it. Half the menu she didn't like, the other half she couldn't understand.

Her father and mother had loved those places and dragged Tracy along a couple of times. All they'd ever ordered was steak, or whatever fancy French term the restaurant happened to call it, which they just as easily could have bought at Sendik's and cooked themselves. A total waste of money and human resources.

Then of course there would be the small issue of staring into Paul Sanders's eyes for over an hour, conversing intelligently about produce. Doubtless she wouldn't be able to eat a thing. Possibly she wouldn't even survive.

She turned the corner onto Juneau Avenue, spotted the restaurant, parked around the corner and slumped down in her seat. This was horrible. This was agony. This would probably be the worst hour of her entire—

Her door opened abruptly and scared her practically to death. She peered up in confusion and saw Paul, one hand on her open door, the other extended.

"May I?"

He grinned down at her, thick hair spilling over his forehead in a boyish unruly way, eyes alive and electric-blue. Tracy's heart lifted and started doing a lovely graceful waltz around her body.

Damn, he was gorgeous.

Damn, she was glad to see him.

Damn.

She grinned back, entirely against her will and put her hand into his nice warm strong one, praying she could get out of her car with half the grace of her waltzing heart. He supported her easily and, magically, her foot didn't get tangled in the seatbelt, nor did she stumble into him and knock them both onto the pavement in the path of an onrushing car. An auspicious beginning to certain torture.

"Your dad coming on his own?"

Tracy closed her door and locked it carefully, wishing she could be spared having to deliver this particular news item. "No. He's...not coming. He was ambushed and held hostage by a shipment of avocados."

"I see." Paul shot her a very, very sexy, amused look that made her blush as she always seemed to do around him and was getting pretty sick of. "So. Alone again."

"Naturally."

He chuckled. "Let's see if we can behave this time."

She gave a careless little laugh and fell into step beside him, wanting to slap herself for even acknowledging the urge to yell, *let's not and see what happens.* "I'm not worried."

"Good. You should be anything but worried in a place like this."

Paul opened the restaurant door. Tracy took a deep breath and walked in, taking in the sophisticated patrons, the terribly restrained decor, the spotless rose-colored tablecloths, tiny pink buds on each table and walls painted the same muted pink as the linens. The overall effect was like being inside a piece of extremely high-class bubble gum.

No worry? Easy for him to say. This place *was* him. All showy plates and fancy glasses and designer food with no real substance. A waste of money. An equal waste of a fabulous-looking man. Hadn't he ever experienced the joy of sucking down a really good cheeseburger at Nate's Place?

They sat at a table against one of the pink walls and the waitress, or whatever you called them in a place like this...*le table attendant?*...handed them enormous menus. Tracy scanned the list of dishes, panic clutching her insides. Not a single normal recognizable anything on the entire list. She slid a glance to the neighboring table just receiving its sacred gift of food and saw entrées presented as if they were works of art. Careful fussy zigzags of multicolored sauces on enormous plates, with a tiny pile of whatever-it-was in the middle, layered in a perfect circle with something green and fuzzy on top.

Help.

She looked back to find Paul studying her over the top of his menu. "See anything you like?"

He asked the question gently, as if he weren't just making chitchat, but really wanted to know.

"Everything looks...amazing." She smiled and bent her head over her menu, trying to find some familiar combination of flavors. Baked chicken with tomato? Spinach lasagna? Spaghetti and meatballs? No dice.

The waitress came back to announce the specials as if she thought the fate of the universe depended on her recitation. "Today Chef Mathilde has prepared monkfish lightly poached in a vegetable broth, served with a shallot champagne sauce garnished with black truffles. She is also offering breast of duck served rare with a reduction sauce and eggplant ravioli on a fresh tomato coulis infused with rosemary and olives."

Paul thanked her and asked for a few more minutes to look over the menu. The waitress inclined her head in solemn acknowledgement and swept away.

Tracy swallowed. *Monkfish? Reduction sauce?*

"Have you been here before?" Paul asked the question in an overly casual tone, which must mean it was totally obvious she hadn't.

She gritted her teeth. "What do you think?"

"Oh, sorry, I forgot." He grinned. "This is the kind of place only parasitic capitalist consumers like me go to."

"That's right."

"Well, Tracy." He folded his menu and slapped it down on the table. "In that case, I think you're in for a surprise."

"Oh, you do." She couldn't hold onto her nice little sense of outrage when he was smiling at her like that. In fact, she couldn't even keep herself from smiling back.

"Will you let me order for you?" He lifted a hand to cut off her scowling protest. "Not because I don't think you're capable, but because I come here a lot and know what's good. Fair enough?"

Tracy gave one last glance at the menu, shrugged and closed it. Okay, she was grateful for the rescue, though not sure if he wanted to lord his knowledge over her or, miracle of miracles, sensed her uneasiness and wanted to relieve her of it. The result was the same. He knew what he was doing and she was horribly out of place. "Fair enough."

"Good." He took her menu and put it on top of his. "Now let's talk about 21st Century tomatoes."

"Okay." She nodded. At least she could converse intelligently on that topic, as long as they stayed away from words like naked and juicy. "Bring me up to date on your end."

"I met with Karen and Jim and we did some brainstorming. Not quite as...interesting as yours and mine, but probably more productive."

His devilish half grin made her laugh. No question, Paul Sanders had the total package. Charm, humor, intelligence, talent and sex appeal that would sway a monkfish from its vows. So why the hell couldn't he also be someone she could take to the farm? Someone who would appreciate its beauty and simplicity, someone who could experience deep satisfaction in finding a perfect red apple on a tree, or the perfect shady spot for a nap on a hot afternoon?

She unfolded her napkin from its origami-like formation and put it into her lap to distract herself from a strange heavy disappointment. "Did you come up with anything?"

"A few ideas, yes. We'll work on them more this week and see if we can present them in a format worth your time. I'll let you know when we're meeting again, though. You can come by anytime."

"Thanks."

"We did decide that—"

"Are you ready to order?" The waitress stood at attention, head cocked coolly to one side.

"Yes." Paul picked up a menu. "The lady will have the quail egg with vodka cream and osetra caviar then the salad with duck. I'll have the tuna tartare and the monkfish. We'll each have a glass of your *Loire Crémant* with the first course, I'll have the Meursault with my fish and she'd like a glass of the '94 Rioja with her duck."

Tracy blinked. *She would?* Of course, she would. Ninety-four *Ree-oh-ha. Yup. Uh-huh. You bet. Woke up this morning with a craving for it, in fact.* Along with *Lwar cray-maw,* whatever the heck that was, and a nice big salad with a duck on it. *Mm-mm good.*

The waitress nodded and swept away from the table without jotting down a word.

Tracy frowned. "Shouldn't she ask if I want fries with that?"

Paul's smile spread slowly across his face until it reached his eyes and they did that sexy crinkling thing at the corners. The look that made her feel like a jewel he'd just discovered in his own backyard, the look that made her feel warm and special and a little gooey and extremely panicked. Because it made *that* happen again. That crazy desire, that crazy need to push closer to the edge, to make something happen between them that shouldn't ever happen.

The waitress arrived with their *Lwar cray-maw*—which turned out to be champagne—just in time to keep Tracy's evil twin from doing anything they'd both regret. Now if she could just turn down the excitement still humming through her body.

Paul clinked their glasses and watched her take her first sip. She kept a polite expression on her face, bracing herself for the thin sour aftertaste of the supermarket brands she bought to celebrate special occasions. Instead, a light spicy wonderfully clean flavor tickled her with unimaginably tiny bubbles that danced all the way down.

"Oh my goodness." She laughed for the sheer pleasure of it. "That's wonderful."

He nodded and she got the impression he was trying hard not to look smug. Immediately she brought her delight under control. "You were telling me about your meeting with Karen and Jim."

"Yes. We want to change the name. 21st Century tomatoes isn't quite...sexy enough."

"Tomatoes have to be sexy?" She beat back the blush creeping up her neck. Impossible to hear "sex" and "tomatoes" without thinking about their encounter the other night, and more impossible to keep that strange hungry part of her from wanting to feel that way again.

He kept his eyes on her over the rim of his champagne glass. "Everything in advertising has to be sexy, which is not the same as sexual. Though that doesn't hurt."

"No." She sipped her bubbly bit of paradise, already feeling its warm swirl through her system. "Sex never hurts."

He put his glass down. "Is that fact or philosophy?"

She fixed her gaze on her plate. "I...was talking about advertising."

Wasn't she? No. She wasn't. She was doing it again. Since when did she crave this kind of cheap stimulation? Yeah, since when. Maybe since she first laid eyes on Paul Sanders.

"Advertising. I see."

"What..." She squeezed her eyes shut for a second to regain control. For the rest of her life she would never drink *Lwar cray-maw* on an empty stomach with the personification of sex appeal sitting opposite. "What do you want to change the name to?"

"We haven't decided." His voice dropped to become decidedly unbusinesslike. "But I think there might have to be some changes, Tracy. Things can't go on the way they are."

Tracy swallowed. Oh my goodness. *Oh my goodness.* "Are *you* talking about advertising?"

"Isn't that what we're always talking about?"

"Of...course." She gave him a weak half smile, feeling trapped in some hormonal net that surrounded them on all sides whenever they were together. "But it might be—"

The waitress put a dish in front of her and Tracy forgot whatever she'd been going to say, if indeed she'd been going to say anything, which in her current state of bewildered arousal was doubtful and probably a good thing. Arranged on the plate in tiny silver egg-cups were three equally tiny black-and-white speckled eggs, about the size of jawbreakers. The tops had been neatly removed and a little ridged collar of whipped cream piped over the opening. A pile of lustrous pearly gray-black caviar sat on the cream.

What the hell was she going to do with this? She glanced at the thin slices of raw tuna on Paul's plate and decided she'd gotten off easy.

Champagne. A big crisp chilly bracing gulp. Then another.

Okay. She could do this.

She picked up the miniature long-handled spoon and dug in, conscious of him watching. Somehow she managed to get a bite arranged containing soft-cooked egg, cream and some caviar, without dumping it all over the plate.

One deep breath and she sent it home.

A burst of contrasting flavors, textures and temperatures erupted in her mouth. Warm rich egg, cool cream with a sharp tang of vodka, salty little popping explosions of the most delicate clean taste she'd ever experienced from the sea.

Heaven. Absolute heaven.

She looked up and met Paul's eyes over the table. He was still trying not to look smug, but wasn't succeeding so well this time. "Good?"

She nodded.

"Try this." He reached for one of her forks and piled up some tuna with a dab of a green stuff, and a dab of a black stuff, then held it out over the table. She made herself reach for the fork, wanting to lean forward and have him feed her, but knowing where that would lead. The tuna was delicious, tender and sweet, not at all fishy, with a mustardy kick from one sauce and a gingery punch from the other.

More heaven.

The waitress came by and, as customary, stood at grave attention, as if she had mechanical parts. "Can I get you anything more?"

Tracy raised a finger. "Ketchup?"

"Ketchup." A cool measuring stare came her way.

"I was kidding." Tracy gestured to her plate. "This is delicious."

"Whew!" The waitress broke into easy natural laughter. "I can never assume anyone is joking. You'd be surprised what we get asked for."

She swept away, still chuckling. Tracy blinked and shook her head. "I didn't expect that."

"What?"

"She was so stuffy before."

"Stuffy?" Paul studied her curiously. "A lot of people are bothered by chatty waitresses. In a place like this they have to be sure the customers are happy. She was just doing her job."

"Oh." Tracy finished her eggs and drained her glass, feeling like the farm girl she was.

"You *do* belong here, you know."

She jerked her head up. "Excuse me?"

Paul leaned forward. "You belong here. So stop trying to convince yourself you don't."

"*You* belong here. I belong at Nate's Place, downtown."

"Why?"

"Because I feel at home there. The burgers are great, the people know me—"

"The food here is great, and if you come often enough they'll know you, too."

She glared at him. Once again, he was totally unable to understand. "Have *you* ever been to Nate's Place?"

"No."

"I rest my case."

"So take me there."

"What?" She burst out laughing at the picture of Mr. Designer Perfection stuffed into a greasy plastic booth, then sobered when she saw he was serious.

"Take me there. Show me. I want to see firsthand how you belong there while you don't at all belong here."

"You wouldn't like it."

"Why not?"

She waved her arm in a frustrated sweep indicating the megabucks ambiance. "It's just hamburgers there."

He sat back in his seat and took a deep breath as if he was trying not to tear his hair out. Or hers. "What makes you think I don't like hamburgers?"

"Maybe you do. But I bet the kind you like come from cows raised on poetry readings and prebreakfast massages."

He turned his head toward the wall and swore. "Tracy, you are bringing out some seriously dangerous urges in me right now."

His deep voice made the words somehow dark and suggestive. Tracy took in a quick breath. Desire rose sharp and hot inside her, fueled by his words and by her champagne. It was happening again and she wanted it to. A strange disembodied sensation swept over her, brightness behind her eyes, a rushing in her ears. The feeling she was watching somebody else, a woman who had the nerve and the increasingly addictive need to push the envelope.

"What kind of dangerous urges?" Her voice came out husky and strange; a thrill ran through her at her own daring. What the hell was she doing? This wasn't like her at all. It was incredibly exciting.

His face stilled and took on an intensity that made her shiver and heat up at the same time. He swung his head slowly up to face her. "We aren't behaving again."

"I'm sorry." But she wasn't.

"I'm not. I don't think you are, either."

"No." She shook her head. "I ought to be, though."

"Maybe you should think less about what you ought to be and more about what you really want."

"Oh, you think so."

"Yes." He leaned forward until the restaurant dimmed to a blurry hum around them. "I'll tell you about my dangerous urges, if you tell me what you really want, Tracy."

You. Omigod, I want you. She crossed her legs and squeezed her thighs tightly together. Something had to give or she'd either explode from frustration, or touch herself right here in public.

She managed an apologetic grin. "Maybe we should go back to talking business."

"Maybe we should talk about what's happening between us so we don't keep getting hijacked by it."

She concentrated on weaving her fingers together, then sent him a mischievous glance. "You first."

"Okay." He cleared his throat. "I thought acknowledging that I was attracted to you would clear the air and we could live with it and get on with business. Apparently I was wrong."

The waitress appeared and took their plates. Tracy raised her eyebrows. "So?"

"So I'm thinking..." He reached across the cleared table and took her hand loosely, ran his finger in a small circle on her palm. "If staying away from you doesn't work to clear the air, maybe something else will."

"Like...what?" She was melting. No, smoldering. No, about to flash into flames any second. Whatever. Hot.

He kept making that slow circle on her hand, mouth barely curving, eyes giving her the message loud and clear.

"Oh. That." The words came out silly and breathless. If she thought she was impossibly hot for him before, now she was...hotter. It was sorely tempting. *He* was tempting. The whole proposition was one giant bowl of super sugar-coated temptation.

Except sugar coating usually disguised the fact that nothing underneath it was any good for you.

She bit her lip. "We're not exactly...well suited."

"I'm not asking you to marry me."

For no reason she could fathom, his comment hurt.

"You mean you want to...be together. To clear the air. Scratch something that itches to make it go away."

He grimaced. "Boy do you have a romantic way with words. I'd rather think of it as a thunderstorm. The pressure builds up, the humidity increases until you can't function, then a fantastic storm sweeps over and everything is peaceful and fresh and calm."

"Be my negatively charged thunderhead, baby?"

He grinned. "Something like that."

"I can't, Paul." She hated the words the minute they left her throat. Damn her stupid practical vulnerable nature. "It's not in my makeup."

"Ever tried?"

She shook her head. Emotional suicide wasn't her idea of a good time. "Not like that."

"Because it seems to me that since I'm obviously so horribly, wretchedly and revoltingly unsuitable, I would be the perfect choice."

"You're assuming I want to try in the first place."

"Don't you?" His smile faded into that intense sexy gaze; he reached his legs out under the table and trapped hers between. "With me? As much as I do with you?"

Yes. Yes. Omigod, yes. And at the exact same time—*No. Forget it. Never.* They'd do the fantastic thunderstorm thing, then he'd have his peaceful fresh calm and she'd have vulnerability and uncertainty and sexually initiated Artificial Attachment Syndrome for someone totally wrong for her.

"Here we are." The waitress arrived with the next course on plates covered by large silver domes. Another waiter positioned himself behind Paul. At some silent signal they lifted the covers with simultaneous flourishes and swished away.

Tracy put on an immensely impressed expression, grateful for the interruption to regain some balance. "Do we applaud?"

"Tracy." He squeezed her legs tightly within his. "Promise me. Promise me you'll consider my...merger offer."

She laughed. "Yes. I'll consider it."

"Good." He relaxed his legs. "Let's eat. And maybe even talk some business at our business lunch."

"It's a deal." Tracy loaded her fork. She knew before she even raised it to her lips that this dish would be delicious, too. Warm crisp bites of duck contrasted with the vinegary sweetness of the salad and the tart pop of fresh currants. A rich melting slice of duck foie gras turned out to be every bit deserving of the hype she'd always heard. The *ree-oh-ha* was complex, mellow—totally unlike any red wine she'd ever tried.

In short, she'd been captivated, totally won over. Seduced by the food, the atmosphere and her companion until she barely recognized herself.

Paul ate his meal in full smug mode, not even trying to look otherwise, and she couldn't bring herself to care. Okay. He won that round. She still had Nate's.

They finished eating, abandoning any pretense at talking about business after a few half-hearted tries, argued amicably over the check, split it and left. Paul walked her to her car and they stood by a newly planted elm that cast only enough shade for her to stand in and enjoy the cool breeze blowing off the lake.

"Next time you come here you should try the sea bass." His voice was carefully casual.

Tracy smiled, ready to admit all-out defeat. "Next time, maybe I will. Thanks."

"Don't mention it." He put his hands to his hips, pushing back his jacket in that way that made his chest wide and available. "And I'm holding you to our date at Nate's Place."

"Did I say it was going to be a date?"

"No, I did."

"Paul." She gestured helplessly. "I don't think—"

He stepped forward. "I know what you don't think, Tracy. You've made it very, very clear what you don't think. But the fact remains we just spent an hour and a half in that restaurant and we talked shop maybe three minutes of that, am I right?"

"Yes," she whispered. "But that's because—"

"I've done all the sensible things so far, I've told myself you're a client and I can't get involved, I've told myself everything possible, but the fact is when I'm with you, the last thing I'm interested in is business and I think it's the same for you."

"Yes." Her voice rose. "Except I have to—"

"So if you don't mind, I'd like to go to Nate's with you, and I'd like it to be a date, and I don't want to talk about anything having to do with tomatoes except the ones on our burgers and I want you to entertain the possibility of coming home with me afterwards. Can you do that?"

"*Yes.* I already said I would. Now will you *please* let me—"

"And one more thing." He moved closer, until they were both in the shade of the little elm. "I would really like it if you would stop twisting your hands and relax that scrunchy thing you have going with your mouth."

She pulled her hands apart and glared at him in total frustration. "Can I please finish a—"

"Thank you."

He leaned down and kissed her full on the mouth, hard and long, the way she used to dream about and practice with her pillow as a girl, but which no man had ever managed to get exactly right.

Paul got it right. Exactly.

Except that it was over much too soon and he was staring at what must be a total dreamy dazed expression on her face and gently brushing curls off her forehead.

"Call me when you're ready to go to Nate's, okay?"

He kissed her briefly again and she stood there in the sun-dappled shade of the little tree next to her car, watching him stride away until he disappeared around the corner.

Doomed? Had she thought she was doomed? Forget doomed. Doomed was manageable. Doomed was fine. She felt nothing but nostalgic affection for doomed.

Because as of right now, she was total, no-holds-barred history.

8

TRACY FLOATED back into 330 East Kilbourn Avenue, wafted up along with the elevator to the ninth floor offices of 21st Century Produce and danced into her suite, not surprised that Mia wasn't back from lunch yet.

Paul wanted her. And she could have him. The fact that following through might be a bad idea was not allowed to enter her fantasies until tonight when she met with the girls. Then she could face reality. Right now she was too busy floating, wafting and dancing her way through the champagne-enhanced afternoon, reliving the firm possessive touch of his mouth, the way-sexy smell of his aftershave, the hard warmth of his body...

She walked around Mia's desk to grab the mail and sort through it. What a time. What a—

"Well, hello."

She looked up from her mail and her fantasies to see one of the hugest men she'd ever laid eyes on filling the suite doorway. He had to be well over six feet and built like a linebacker, dark and very attractive in an obvious sort of way.

"I'm Dave. And you are..." He peered at Mia's nameplate. "Mia Templeton."

"Actually, I'm—"

"Mee-a." He practically purred the name, inasmuch as an enormous bass voice could purr. "In Italian it means...mine."

He accompanied the words with a dark stare so melting that Tracy's jaw shot open in sheer awe. *Whew!* This guy must drop 'em like flies.

"I wonder, Mee-a, if you could tell me where I might find the lovely and talented Tracy Richards."

"Right here."

He blinked. "You?"

She nodded and couldn't stop a snort of laughter at the surprise on his face. "Can I help you?"

"I think you can."

Again that deep purr, like rich fur sliding over bare skin. Or something. Tracy suppressed another snort. The man was a major pro. "Shoot."

"I think you know my best buddy, Paul Sanders."

Tracy received this news with a gasp. Unfortunately, she also happened to be swallowing at the same time, so she got to spend a lovely minute or so nearly choking to death.

"Easy there." He patted her gently on the back with a huge hand. "Easy. If you die I'd feel responsible."

"Why...are you here?" She managed a full breath and bent her head gratefully, hand still at her throat.

He wandered over to the wall and examined the watercolor landscapes Tracy had chosen for her office. "I want to take you to dinner tomorrow."

Tracy's head shot up. *He did?* "You do?"

"Yeah. Since Paul is in love with you, I figured—"

"What?" Tracy clutched her chest. Dave sprang up to the desk, hand ready for more back pats, but she managed to gasp and swallow in the proper sequence this time. "He *told* you that?"

"Oh, no." Dave waved a finger back and forth. "No, no, no. He doesn't even *know* it yet. Just me."

Tracy fell back into Mia's chair so hard it rolled half-way to the wall behind it. This encounter was already exhausting. And for one weird surreal moment—dis-appointing. Which made no sense. Why would she want Paul to be in love with her? She wouldn't. Because of course that would only confuse things more.

"So why does Paul being in...why does that make you want to take me to dinner?"

"Two reasons." He cleared his throat. "One, I have something of a...reputation with the ladies."

Now that she could believe. "Really."

He shrugged. "When the right one comes along I'll be as devoted and faithful as they come. But right now, why bother? Get out there and live, that's what I say. You know what I mean?"

"Uh...yeah." She tried not to think about that particular philosophy in terms of her and Paul. Just because she wasn't out there screwing around didn't mean she wasn't *living*. "But what does this have to do with—"

"I figure since Paul keeps insisting you mean nothing to him, then he's not going to mind if I take you out, right?" He winked and tapped the side of his forehead. "But I know better. Since you actually mean everything to him, once he's faced with the fact that someone like me, who is generally...successful with the ladies, has you in his company for an evening, he'll be forced to acknowledge his deep and abiding love for you."

"He will." The logic was definitely escaping her.

"In short, he'll go nutso jealous."

"I...see." She scootched the chair close to Mia's desk and picked up her mail again. Dave might be charming, but he was also apparently manipulative. She doubted very much that Paul would appreciate this kind of help with his...lust life. "And reason two?"

"Reason two, I think you don't have the total picture that is Paul Sanders. I don't think *he* has the total picture that is Paul Sanders, or at least he's hidden it temporarily. And I'd like to share that with you. You should see it."

"Oh." She put the mail down again and folded her hands together in her lap. She didn't much admire the "make him nutso jealous" part of the plan, but the honest affection and concern on Dave's face when he talked about his friend made the rest of the idea much more appealing. Who wouldn't want an insider's view of someone as confusing as Paul? Maybe Dave could help her sort him out.

"And reason three..."

She frowned. "I thought there were only two."

"The third one goes without saying. You are beautiful and I want to take you to dinner. And four..."

"Four?"

He gave her another killer smile. "I'm having cravings."

Tracy shrank back. "Cravings."

"Serious cravings. For meat. Ground meat. On a

bun. And there's only one place in this beertown to go when you crave ground meat on a bun." He winked and leaned over the desk as if he was going to impart a solemn secret.

She grinned at his handsome easygoing face and opened her mouth, certain they were going to say the exact same thing at the exact same time.

"Nate's Place."

"SO I SAID I'D GO." Tracy shrugged and sipped at her water. Her blissful high of the afternoon had faded into headache and uncertainty. Should she go to Nate's with Dave? Should she go to Nate's with Paul? Should she talk to Dave? Should she sleep with Paul? Yes? No? Should she? Shouldn't she?

This was ridiculous.

Allegra, Cynthia and Missy stared at her around their table at Louise's.

"Let me get this straight." Cynthia leaned forward onto clasped hands. "You're going out with this Dave guy to make Paul jealous?"

"I don't think that's right." Missy gave a worried frown. "That stuff always backfires in the end."

"No, no, no." Tracy held up both hands. "I'm not *going out* with him. I'm just going...out with him. The jealousy thing was his idea. I definitely don't think that will work."

"Ha!" Cynthia slapped her palm on the table. "Then you don't know men. They're like little territorial pit bulls. Even if they *don't* want you, they sure as hell don't want their best friend having you. And we know for sure Paul wants you. Trust me, he'll go ape."

"Dave isn't going to *have* me. He wants to tell me something about Paul and I...think I might want to hear." She took a deep breath against irrationally threatening tears. Somewhere along the way she'd decided to give Paul a chance and it was obviously scaring her to death since she was ready to cry every time his name was mentioned.

Maybe Dave wouldn't give her more than a hyped-up sales pitch, but there was always hope that her guy radar hadn't malfunctioned as severely as she thought. That it hadn't pointed her in such an entirely wrong direction. Maybe she and Paul could find some common ground. After all, even though they'd grown in opposite directions, they'd both started out humbly, both come into money later in their lives. And look how much she'd liked eating quail eggs and duck salad.

"I don't like it." Allegra shook her head so her six-inch multihoop earrings smacked her repeatedly on the cheeks. "Why don't you go to the source? If you want to know about Paul, then ask Paul."

Tracy rolled her eyes. "Ask him what? 'Gee, Paul, I sense that everything you've shown me about yourself is complete and utter bull. Would you mind revealing your true inner nature?'"

"Oh." Allegra wrinkled her nose. "I see what you mean."

"I still think you should come clean about knowing he was impersonating Dan at the shore. Especially if he..." Missy cleared her throat and blushed. "Seems to want to...uh—"

"Do you like a crazed orangutan."

"Cynthia!" Missy hunkered down in her seat.

Tracy studied her interlocked fingers. "I still think the confession has to come willingly, not be forced by me confronting him. Maybe after I talk to Dave that will all make sense, too."

"Well, well." Cynthia raised her eyebrows. "I sense a real change of heart in progress."

"I think maybe your heart has already changed." Allegra reached out and squeezed Tracy's hand. Missy nodded.

Oh no. This time the irrational tears came irrationally up into Tracy's eyes, rolled irrationally down her cheeks and dripped all over the innocent napkin in her lap. Then more tears. A regular mortifying irrational waterfall.

The girls immediately mobilized tissues, in Missy's case a cotton monogrammed handkerchief, and passed them over. Tracy blew her nose on the tissues and dabbed at her eyes with the hanky. "My lord, I'm a nutcase over this man. What is happening to me?"

"You're in love." Missy's face glowed with gooey-eyed happiness that made Tracy shudder, except she couldn't tell if it was a fear-and-loathing type shudder or an eerie-excitement shudder. Or both.

Had she mentioned this was ridiculous?

"Come on, Missy. How could I be in love? I barely know the man and I don't respect his choices or his lifestyle." The denials leaped out of her mouth. "Can you picture him enjoying life on our farm?"

"Sounded to me a minute ago like you were way open to revising your opinion of his choices. And as for the farm..." Cynthia rolled her eyes.

"What about the farm?"

"The farm is a nice place, Tracy, but it's not paradise like you keep talking about."

Tracy bristled. "Maybe not to you. I was a hell of a lot happier there. If my dad didn't need me here, I'd go back in a second."

"You could be happy here, too, you're just not letting yourself be."

"Cynthia." Allegra laid a restraining hand on her shoulder.

Cynthia fell back against her chair. "I know, I know, shut my mouth. I'm sorry. Sometimes *I* feel like things were simpler in North Carolina and I do miss that. But I sure as hell don't want to go back to that life. Not after I've worked so hard to get this far."

Tracy smiled at her friend, pitying her a little. Cynthia had indeed worked hard. So hard that she still felt the need to deny where she'd come from. As if poverty and shame would suck her back if she acknowledged her past.

"How do you feel when you're around him?" Allegra squeezed lime into her soda water, peering over her bright red half glasses.

Tracy considered, then let out an involuntary, slightly hysterical giggle. "Horny."

Cynthia burst out laughing. "Atta girl."

"But horny isn't love." Tracy put up a protesting hand. "It's just...horny."

"What else? You must feel something else." Allegra dropped the squeezed lime into her drink. "Dig deep inside and remember."

"Well, he is funny and charming. And at the restaurant when he saw I was a little intimidated by the menu, he offered to order for me. That was nice."

"Do you feel different around him? More yourself?" Allegra shrugged. "More like somebody else?"

Tracy swallowed and let out a long sigh. "At the restaurant. At the end. I...didn't feel so out of place. I guess there was that. And..."

"And?" Three heads leaned closer to her around the table.

"I felt...bolder."

"Bolder how?" Cynthia asked.

"...sexually. I mean I said things that...it was like I was someone else."

Missy covered her ears. "I don't think I want to hear this."

Cynthia yanked her hands down. "Yes you do."

"Don't you see?" Allegra reached and patted Tracy's arm. "You feel safe with him. You can let parts of yourself out that no one else has seen."

Tracy's arm tensed under Allegra's soothing pats. She had this immediate crazy urge to cry again, so she laughed instead. "Well that sounds pretty dramatic."

"But you know what, Tracy?" Cynthia leaned forward. "Even I'm in on this one. You got it really bad for this guy. And you'd be an idiot not to go for it."

"Wait a second, let's not go too far." Missy made a time-out *T* with her hands. "That's exactly why she *shouldn't* 'go for it.' She loves him. She could get hurt. Men don't think about sex the same way we do."

"Speak for yourself." Cynthia winked. "Worst thing happens, she has a great time in the sack, it doesn't work out, and she cries for a day or two. Worst case. If his best friend thinks Paul's in love with her, then there's a chance he is. I say do it. Talk to the best friend first. Then call Paul, feed him Nate's burgers and go home with him. Then be sure to call the Manhunters in the morning and tell us all the good stuff."

Allegra held up a finger. "But I agree with Missy, you need to clear up the business at the shore first. You can't enter into this—"

"Or let *him* enter into you..."

Allegra smacked Cynthia's shoulder. "You can't get involved with him with any kind of deception still brewing. It'll screw up your karma from the beginning."

"I agree."

Tracy looked around the table at the three women. She'd come here for advice and she'd gotten it. And by the excitement burgeoning up from under her superficial protests, it was exactly what she wanted to hear. Hadn't the Manhunters made a pledge to explore this kind of chemistry? Wasn't she aching for more of that addictive thrill of being with him? Yes, she could get hurt, but maybe Dave did know something about Paul's true feelings. Maybe by being with him, she'd find out that—

Tracy scowled. To hell with reason. To hell with justification. The whole tangle boiled down to the fact that she wanted to be in Paul Sanders's bed more than she didn't.

She'd go to dinner with Dave, find out what he had to say, then call Paul...and for once in her life, in Cynthia's immortal words: go for it.

PAUL JIGGLED his key in the lock on his condo door, arms full of files, jacket slung over his elbow, mail clenched between his teeth. Hell of a day. Seven-thirty, no dinner yet, hadn't had time to go to the gym, didn't have time to now.

He turned the key, pushed open the door and shut it behind him with his foot. The smell of cleaning fluid met his nose. Sue must have been in today; the place was immaculate.

For one head-clouding second, he imagined the house smelling of dinner and Tracy. Imagined her home already or expected soon, greeting him with a peck on the cheek.

Hi, honey, how was your day?

He shook his head and changed the picture. No. Tracy greeting him in a sexy little black dress that showed off her fair skin and slender figure.

No. In a lace bra and panties under a white transparent robe.

Uh-uh. Totally naked spread-eagled on his bed, her dark curls contrasting with the white cotton of his pillowcases and her darker curls contrasting with the white skin of her thighs.

He shut his eyes and dumped the files on his kitchen counter so he could adjust himself under his pants. Man, had she ever gotten into his system. Even on one of his nightmare busy days he didn't go more than twenty minutes without thinking about her and whether she'd take him up on his offer. Didn't answer one phone call without hoping it was her. She had his damn balls in a sling.

He pressed the playback button on his answering machine and opened the refrigerator, scowling at the contents. Half a pot of fennel leek soup, *Pol Roger* champagne, marinated asparagus...nothing appealed. Tonight he was in the mood for some serious meat and potatoes.

Beep. The answering machine clicked into action. He kept scanning the refrigerator, but stopped registering what he saw. Had Tracy left one of the messages? Even knowing she didn't have his home number didn't keep him from hoping.

"Hi Paul, it's Mom. Just calling to say hi. I know you're busy. Love you." *Beep.*

"Paul, it's John, gimme a call sometime, we can play golf." *Beep.*

"Yo, *Paul.*" Dave's voice boomed over the machine. "You didn't call me back."

Paul winced and pushed aside a bag of Belgian endive. He'd tried once, then the day had overtaken him.

"Remember how you said you weren't interested in Tracy?"

Paul straightened and turned to stare at the answering machine, as if watching it would prepare him better for whatever Dave was about to say.

"Well, I wanted to talk to you first, but you didn't call back. In any case, I stopped by her office yesterday and met her." He whistled suggestively.

Paul shut the refrigerator.

"I figured since you weren't into her, you wouldn't mind if I asked her out."

Paul took three steps toward the machine.

"I wanted to clear it with you first, but it kind of happened fast. I'm taking her out tonight. To Nate's."

Nate's. Paul recoiled as if Dave's fist had made contact with his midsection; his muscles bunched instinctively for counterattack.

What the hell is this, Dave?

"Just wanted you to know. See you around buddy."

The machine beeped and clicked off. Paul put his hand to his forehead. *Okay, think.* Dave was trying to make him jealous. Part of his ludicrous She's-The-One matchmaking plan. In fact, Dave had probably left the message with information about where they were precisely to make Paul show up at Nate's in some crazed caveman rage, demanding his woman. *Well, think again, Dave.* Paul wasn't that easily manipulated.

He dropped his hands to his hips. *Be rational.* Nothing was going to happen tonight. Dave was far too good a friend and far too honorable a person to take advantage of the situation. He'd take Tracy out, they'd talk, Dave would keep one eye on the door for Caveman Paul and that would be the end of it. Even as much as Dave loved scoring, he'd control himself this time. For Paul's sake. For sure.

Right. Paul clapped his hands together. Nothing to worry about. It was actually nice that Tracy wanted to get to know Paul's friends. Really nice. He could picture her and Dave hanging out together in comfortable, casual clothes, chatting amicably, easily over their burgers. Maybe even right then, Tracy was laughing at something Dave said.

Paul smiled to himself at the thought. See? He could picture that no problem. Tracy sitting opposite his best friend. Laughing.

Her eyes came alive like nothing he'd ever seen when she laughed. It was as if she opened up to let someone else through. In those moments he realized how muted and sad she was the rest of the time.

Now Dave was probably doing that for her. Making her happy. Making her laugh. Dave was a funny guy. Charming. Irresistible.

He moved his jaw which for some reason had set itself painfully rigid. Good! That was good. Tracy needed to be happy more often. He'd like to make her that happy all the time, keep her eyes that alive. As alive as they were when she baited him at Chez Mathilde, said those tantalizing things, her breath as high as her color, trembling a little as if she was taking her life into her hands for the first time and finding the danger well worth it.

At that moment, his brain turned inside out, his body rock hard under the tablecloth, he'd realized how ludicrous it was to pretend to himself or anyone else that his feelings for Tracy were either platonic or easily controlled. At that moment he'd decided that he wanted her in bed and damn the consequences.

He forced his fists to unclench. *Relax, relax.* She wouldn't take that same sensual risk with Dave. Just because Dave had picked her favorite restaurant, where she'd be at ease and at home, while Paul took her to the fussiest place in town, knowing she'd be way out of her element. He'd tried so hard to impress her with his class without thinking of her comfort. While Dave...Dave knew.

Freaking Nate's Place.

And the damn irony was that Dave had never seen a day's deprivation in his life.

Paul stalked into his bedroom, unbuttoned his Thomas Pink shirt, bunched it and threw it on the bed. Fine. Terrific. Dave's stupid, transparent, manipulative little piece of bullshit had worked. Paul was like a helpless guppy caught in a tidal undertow.

He pulled off his undershirt and yanked down his suit pants, opened his bottom drawer and rummaged around until he came up with a pair of jeans and his Attitude! T-shirt. She wanted Nate's? Fine. She'd get it. But not with Dave, damn him all to hell.

He kicked off his Prada dress shoes, tossed his Tse socks over his shoulder and pulled on plain cotton sport socks and his beat-up hiking boots. She was going to spend the evening at Nate's with *him.* He was going to eat her precious hamburgers, bring her back home and start their relationship back at square one. Come clean about the Dan charade and indulge every spark of their electric attraction as he should have that first night on the beach at Fish Creek.

And if he had anything to say about it, she'd end up feeling as helpless and guppylike in the face of this powerful passion as he did.

9

PAUL PULLED UP to the curb and parked down the block from Nate's Place on Bradbury street, got out and slammed his door.

"Nice car." The cocky voice came from behind him.

The old reflexes took over. Paul swung around, careful to keep his movements casual, not threatening, not defensive. A group of teenagers, all shapes, sizes and colors, sat clustered on the gray cement front steps of an apartment building, elbowing each other and snickering. He forced his body to relax. Reminded himself he was nearly old enough to be their father. Reminded himself they weren't laughing at anything he was ashamed of. How many times had he sat outside with his friends on hot summer evenings like this, dreaming up ways to get into trouble? Mostly harmless stuff. No threat.

"Thanks." He glanced back at his prized possession, his gold Lexus ES300, and suddenly saw it through their eyes. Stuffy. Pretentious. The kind of car Paul's dad would drive his new wife to charity balls in. Right now the kids were probably making the same kind of assumptions about Paul.

He pressed his keyless entry system to lock, and strode toward Nate's, past tired gray buildings and blowing dust, trying not to care what a bunch of teenagers thought, feeling cold inside in spite of the August heat. None of them knew he'd grown up like them. They probably assumed he'd been driving a car like that since he got his license. Some might envy him; some might scorn him; some both.

The muscles at the back of his neck tightened. Maybe one of them was still watching him, with a particularly determined look in his eye. Maybe that kid would vow to own a Lexus someday and work like crazy until he did. A moment like this could change a kid's life if he wanted it badly enough. Paul remembered that moment for him, when Alan Dirkson had driven his Alpha Romeo convertible off into the bright sunshine of prestige with Paul's teenage dream goddess, Samantha Leberman beside him, leaving Paul, impotent and seething on the sidewalk.

He hadn't made a conscious vow then to succeed. Nothing that dramatic. But he'd been driven to work his ass off in some vague and ill-formed plan of revenge until he discovered his talent and charted a concrete course toward where he wanted to be.

Except sometimes he wasn't sure exactly where that was.

He reached Nate's and flung open the door, went inside to the clamor and blast of the barely working air conditioner. The distantly familiar greasy fried smell seemed to coat his nostrils and lungs within seconds. He tried to block out the noise and the odor and the tacky feel of the place. If he wasn't so damn hungry and grouchy he'd drive Tracy to the Lake Park Bistro for some decent food.

Where was she?

He heard her laughing and turned to see her leaning forward in a booth toward Dave, hand dipping into a carton of French fries. Something turned over and lifted inside his chest. She lit the place up. Like a queen, like a movie star. What the hell had she meant she belonged here? Her stylish, sweet vulnerability didn't fit this place at all.

"Well, look who's here." Dave's smug tone rang out over the air conditioner and chatter.

Tracy turned and froze with a French fry halfway to her mouth. Then her gaze went up and down, no doubt trying to take in his total lack of Armani. Paul walked to the table and slid into the grimy yellow booth next to her, unable to keep a grin off his lips.

"Hello, Tracy." He kept his voice as low and intimate as he could in the bright lights and noise and was gratified to see her blush and sway toward him slightly. She hadn't fallen under Dave's spell, of course. Paul probably could have stayed home. But damned if he'd been able to keep away from her.

"Imagine running into *you* here." Dave folded his arms across his beefy chest. "*What* a coincidence. And we were just talking about you, too."

"Oh?" He put his arm along the back of the booth behind Tracy and grimaced when his hand encountered something cold and sticky.

"Can you believe this?" Dave shook his head. "A

woman out with me, and you're all she wants to talk about. I must be losing my touch."

Tracy's hands went into her lap and wove together. She dared glance at Paul, the blush heightened on her cheeks, her eyes bright and enticing. Without thinking, he moved close; she turned, surprised, and he kissed her, tasting salt and sweet. He drew back, meaning to smile, but a solemn, still feeling came over him and he couldn't do anything but stare into her startled brown eyes like a lovesick sap, feeling overwhelmed and a little awed.

Holy moly.

"S-o-o-o, I can tell when I'm not wanted. Tracy, it's been a pleasure." Dave heaved his body out of the booth, tipped a fake hat and winked. "Don't be too hard on this guy. See you around."

He walked out, satisfaction radiating from every inch of his enormous body. Paul gave a snort of laughter and shook his head.

"What's so funny?"

"Dave." He stroked back her hair from the side of her face, let his fingers linger on her cheek. "He brought you here to make me jealous."

"He *told* you that?" She stared at him in horror.

"Dave works in mysterious ways." He shrugged. "Is that why you came? To make me jealous?"

He waited for her answer, not sure what he wanted it to be. He wasn't into women who played mind games, but at the same time he didn't exactly love the idea of her so easily accepting invitations from other men.

"No." She shook her head emphatically. "I came because he said he wanted to talk to me about you."

"I see." He kept the relief and sudden wariness out of his voice. "You couldn't come to me with what you wanted to find out?"

She bit her lip. "I should have, I'm sorry. But sometimes friends know us better than we know ourselves. I guess I was curious about Dave's perspective."

"Now there's a frightening thought." He tried to grin, but it didn't work well. He also tried, almost as unsuccessfully, not to feel hurt that she didn't trust his own perspective, didn't feel she could ask him what she wanted to know. "Anything interesting to report?"

The second the words were out of his mouth, he wanted them back. Whatever Dave had talked to her about, he wasn't ready to hear on an empty stomach with half his brain distracted by her and the other by the greasy ambiance.

"Plenty." She addressed this comment to her half-finished meal. Paul went from wary to alarmed. Had Dave spilled the beans about Dan? Made Paul look a liar before he had the chance to clear it up himself?

"Did it work, by the way?" She threw him a coy little sideways glance that made him want to kiss her again.

"What?"

"Were you jealous?"

He turned her face toward him and kissed her again, hard this time and possessively—Caveman Paul marking his territory—then waited for her to look smug and powerful.

She frowned and scrunched her mouth. "That's what he said would happen."

"I'd kiss you?"

"No, that you'd be jealous."

"You didn't believe him?"

She shook her head.

"Oh, Tracy." He kissed her again and became acutely aware that he wanted this damn meal over as soon as possible. "If I wasn't ready to drop from hunger I'd take you home right now and show you."

She looked up at him and he saw the dark excitement starting in her eyes. He grinned and pushed himself out of the booth, holding up his hands as if to shield himself. "Don't look at me like that until I'm sitting down again. I'm going to get some food."

"Need help ordering?" She blinked innocently. "Not because I don't think you're capable, but because I come here all the time and I know what's good."

He laughed, hearing his words to her at Chez Mathilde shot right back at him. "Okay. Help me out with this menu."

"You want the three-course meal. One, cheeseburger deluxe, with the works. Two, fries. Three, chocolate milkshake. Simple."

He nodded and got in line, jostled by someone pushing his way out, jostled again by someone going up to the counter for extra ketchup.

How often had coming to burger joints like this been a special longed-for childhood treat? God, what a lifetime ago. He and his mom alone, Mom's face as she concentrated carefully and counted out exact change.

She always had exact change. As if she was paid in singles and coins, which in retrospect, probably wasn't far from the truth.

He scanned the menu, posted in red plastic letters on a backlit neon board, half of them missing. Che-burg-r De-uxe. Fr-es. Milkshak-. He was getting indigestion already.

How could people eat this way all the time and function? Taste buds in arrested development from the salt-fat monotone of flavors. Bodies flabby and hearts clogged. Stomach bloating from the combination of ice cream and entrée eaten together.

His turn to order. He mumbled out his designated choices, extracted his wallet and paid with a twenty. Then waited for his order, wishing he could get take-out and whisk Tracy back to his clean, quiet, orderly apartment, wondering if they'd laugh if he asked for bottled water. He could already feel the salty thick coating this kind of food brought to the back of his throat.

"Number twenty-*seven*."

He handed over his ticket and took his tray back to Tracy's table, slid in the booth across from her, feeling like a kid in a strange school lunchroom. Familiar routine. New experience.

She smiled in delighted anticipation. "Now. Eat."

He unwrapped the burger from its greasy paper, feeling heat steaming through the spongy bun, enclosing a large thin circle of beef from who knew what parts of the cow.

One bite, with half the toppings trying to slide out the back all over the table, and it all came back.

Salty. Sweet. Juicy. Rich. But more than just the satisfying taste. The feeling. Back in time on a special occasion meal with his mom. As if they were on an adventure. As if they'd taken on the world together and right then, they were winning. Cocooned in a booth, giggling and ketchup-smeared, telling stories about their days, dreaming of their bright fantasy future.

French fries, crisp and salty, thick sweet chocolate shake, who cared if you had dessert before dinner was over? He was hooked now, ravenous, eating up his childhood memories and damn the gas later.

The door opened behind him and three young men came in, shouting a greeting to two guys at a table who shouted back and held up hands for high fives all around. The huge bald man behind the counter waved and yelled out hello, how are you, how's things.

Paul stopped chewing. On his childhood street in Roxbury, Mass, everyone knew everyone else. Restaurants like this were a meeting place, a place to support each other, to feel part of a community. His vision of the meal with his mom opened, widened, to include greetings, salutations, various chats with neighbors and friends. Mrs. Darby and her large brood and larger stomach; old Mr. Hopkins who lived downstairs with a bowlful of goldfish and a hamster named Sweetie; Doris Andrews, whose husband left her for another man, and on and on and on.

In his Shorewood apartment building, besides Dave, he knew no one.

"Is it good?"

He looked across the table at Tracy, nodded and swallowed. He wanted to say something funny and entertaining to make her laugh like Dave had, but just then he couldn't.

Her eyes softened in a way he'd never seen them soften before and she reached across the table and squeezed his arm. "I'm glad you like it."

He put down his food, feeling suddenly phony and cut adrift and ashamed. She deserved so much more than he'd given her. "Did you know it was me last month at the beach? That I was Dan?"

She cast her eyes down, but kept her hand on his arm. "Yes."

God, what an ass he'd been. "How long have you known?"

"Since your presentation to 21st Century."

He sank lower. What a cocky son-of-a-bitch, thinking he could teach her about values—by lying, no less. Assuming if he put on a silk suit he'd be totally unrecognizable, totally transformed. He suppressed a cynical laugh. Looked like he needed the lessons himself.

But then...he hadn't counted on the person Tracy was turning out to be. And he damn well hadn't counted on how he'd come to feel about her.

"So why the hell are you still sitting with me?"

She met his eyes full on. Her mouth opened a couple of times then closed, as if she was afraid of what she was going to say. "Because...I can't seem to stay away from you."

His body reacted immediately. He reached over the narrow table and took her arms. "Tracy."

"Yes." She was whispering, her eyes dark with nervous anticipation and excitement.

"Will you come home with me?" Now he was whispering; the words meant to carry across the table barely made it out of his throat. "Right now?"

She nodded.

They got up and threw away their unfinished meal, pushed out the doors and into the summer evening air. He took her shoulders, swung her around and against the side of the building, kissed her once, kissed her again, and made himself stop before he got sloppy and passionate in public.

"Did Dave drive you here?"

She nodded, eyes alight, skin soft, smooth and pale against her dark eyes and hair.

He took her hand and led her down the street, relieved she wasn't going to have to follow him in her own car. He didn't want her away from him for a second. Not until they'd been together in his bed, and he'd seen her eyes wide and glazed with pleasure.

"You the man!" A chorus of teenage whistles followed the shout.

Paul groaned silently. The group of boys who'd greeted him when he pulled up were scattered defiantly on his Lexus, sitting, leaning, crouched on the roof. This was all he needed.

"Keeping my car warm?" He put his hands to his hips, unsmiling, but kept his tone light, making sure Tracy was slightly behind him and close. Maybe the hamburger had brought back some good memories, but it couldn't erase the bad ones. Every last damn day had been a struggle, to dominate, to survive.

The teenagers laughed in that teenage wiseass voice-cracking way and exchanged cocky glances.

"You want us off?" A handsome kid with shaggy blond hair and a ball cap turned backwards shrugged, arms crossed, hands in his armpits.

"That's right." Paul nodded, held his ground. The boy glanced at his friends, sized up Paul, trying to decide how far to push it.

Come on, kid, back down. It's not worth it.

"Okay. I guess we could do that." The kid slid down off the car. The others followed reluctantly and pushed past Paul and Tracy, deliberately jostling them, the leader nearly knocking Tracy down.

Paul grabbed his arm, and pulled him around. "Your mom not teach you to say excuse me?"

"My mom's dead." He tossed the phrase out.

Paul's gut twisted. "I'm sorry."

The boy's blue eyes narrowed, his stubbled upper lip curled in disgust. "Yeah, right, Lexus Boy."

Words poured into Paul's brain in an eager Dudley-Do-Right rush. *I grew up in a neighborhood like this. I was just like you at your age. You can get out if you want to.* He stopped them in time, realizing how ludicrous they would sound. But they were just what he'd wanted to hear at this kid's age. Just the kind of message he craved and never got.

Or maybe it was just what he wanted to believe about himself back then. If some grown-up with a

Lexus had charged onto his street and told him he could do anything he set his mind to, Paul would probably have socked him in the nose.

He loosened his grip and let the kid push him roughly away to save face in front of his buddies. Who was Paul kidding? Did he think he could charge in for a quick rescue, change lives overnight? He'd spent the past ten plus years working for himself, earning for himself, spending on himself, indulging only himself and his own fantasy of success. Turned his back on where he came from, blocked out the memories of how it had felt to be young and "disadvantaged" as they were so fond of calling it. Hell, he was even scared to death of a burger joint.

He'd also cut himself off from any chance to inspire kids like these to something better.

The boys sauntered away, whooping, yelling obscenities, banging windows and trash cans. Paul watched them, heavy with the remembered aimlessness of his youth. He'd probably pushed them into doing something worse than sitting on a car, to pump their deflated egos back up.

"Paul?"

He turned to see Tracy behind him, eyes wide and anxious. "Are you all right?

He nodded. "Sorry about that."

"It's okay. You handled it well." She bit her lip, didn't meet his eyes.

The heaviness dragged him lower. The evening had been spoiled, the rushing momentum into their night of physical exploration defeated. Tracy wasn't a product of city culture; the encounter had upset her. And this crystal ball glance into Paul's own childhood made it doubtful he could go back to resting easy in his new life now, in the new skin he'd carefully constructed around himself. He might not belong here anymore, but he didn't really belong anywhere else, either.

"Come on. I'll drive you home."

She looked up at him, a little frown drawing her eyebrows down. "My home? Or your home?"

"Yours." He couldn't lighten the dullness in his tone, couldn't lengthen the curt syllable even knowing it might hurt her. "Isn't that what you want?"

She slid her small beautiful hands up his arms to his elbows and held him there, half like a mother who knows her child is in need, half like a lover exploring new skin.

"No," she whispered. "No. It isn't what I want."

TRACY HUNG BACK, helpless and silent, feeling totally useless as Paul put his key into the lock and opened his condo door. Whatever had happened back there, whatever demons had been unleashed in him, she was powerless to understand, powerless to heal him. For that one movie-scene moment when he'd confronted the gang of kids, she felt he'd made contact with the real Paul. That he'd brought out of hiding the man who lurked under all the designer outerwear, a transition begun when he'd tasted that first awesome bite of a Nate's burger and gone off into a trance of memories she hadn't dared intrude on.

According to Dave, Tracy had been right on one

count: the story Paul offered on the beach was the real story of his childhood. His mother raised him alone in a tough part of Boston. He'd made it his goal to escape, and he had.

But there was a difference between escaping to something better and denying your past. How could you be a complete person if you denied your origins and said *sayonara* to the first two decades of your life? Today he'd begun to let those decades back, starting by allowing his body to come into contact with denim. But he was still struggling to form what Dave had called "the total picture that was Paul Sanders."

And she didn't know how to help. Except she knew she could do more here with him, in his bed or out of it, than she could by allowing him to drive her home. Besides, she'd spend the whole night pacing her room worrying about him.

She followed him into his perfect apartment and watched him glance around with tired eyes, wondering if he saw his surroundings now as she did. As a bandage. A fancy gilded bandage, to cover who he was and where he came from.

"Want some decaf? Tea?" He stood, hands on his hips, expression indescribably weary, not even trying to smile.

"No. Thanks."

"Tracy." He swayed toward her, then shifted and held his ground. "I don't know if I can—"

"It's okay." She stepped close to him and pushed her hands up his chest, showing him with her eyes that she was sincere. "It's okay. We can just talk."

He nodded and took her hand. "Come here."

He led her to the sofa where they'd drank wine and brainstormed themselves into sexual heat over tomatoes, and sank down, pulling her into his lap. She curled forward and rested her head on his shoulder, closed her eyes and savored the warm comforting feel of his arms around her. This she could get used to. God only knew if she'd get the chance.

"Want to talk it out?"

"I don't know." He stroked her hair, then let his hand fall heavily to his side. "I don't know."

"Try?" She gave him a coaxing smile and grinned when he managed a smile of his own that brought some life back into his eyes. What she wouldn't give to help bring the rest of it back.

"Those kids." He dragged his hands over his face. "Brought back some memories I wasn't expecting."

"I thought so."

"Dave filled you in, I take it?"

She nodded and carefully pitched her voice to keep it from sounding reproachful. "You could have told me."

"I did tell you. On the beach that night."

"You're right." She grimaced. But she'd been so anxious to condemn him back then, it didn't matter that he'd told the truth. "Then you changed your story."

"I figured it was what you wanted to believe about me—what you already did." He let his head fall back on the sofa. "At that point I had this arrogant idea that I could teach you to value me in spite of the trappings."

She bit her lip and traced a tiny circle around an upholstery button. "I think you did."

He turned toward her without raising his head and gave a tired smile that made her heart melt into Cheez Whiz. "Yeah?"

"Yeah." She whispered the word, trying not to let her goopy tenderness show too much in case it scared him.

He lifted his head and looked down at her, reached and drew his fingers across her mouth. She stared into his blue-gray gaze, his touch lingering on her lips, and felt as if she was disappearing. Slowly, inevitably, the atmosphere changed around them. The light and purpose came back into his eyes; the air between their bodies seemed suddenly charged and alive.

"Tracy." He leaned forward and kissed her, brushed his lips gently across hers, no pressure, no passion; testing, tasting, transmitting the warmth of his mouth to hers. She let him take his time, let him set the pace and the direction, trying to control the simmering emotion threatening to erupt through her. He needed her strength, not her vulnerability.

"Tracy." His hand came up and cupped the back of her head, he deepened the kiss and pulled her more firmly onto his lap, circling her with his arms so that she felt totally enclosed.

She gave herself over to the kiss, wanting him to have her if that's what he chose, wanting to give him whatever he sought in whatever way she could. Never mind she might end this evening with her heart in his hands. He needed her.

"It's good between us."

She laughed, a breathless uneasy sound. "You think?"

"Yes." He pushed her off his lap, stood and bent to scoop her up into his arms. "And I think it could be better."

He carried her into his bedroom, laid her on his bed and stood beside it. Without a trace of self-consciousness, he pulled off his shirt, exposing the broad chest and powerful shoulders she'd spent so much time imagining. He tossed the shirt on the bed and undid his pants, pulled them down and off, all the while looking at her with a smile that was half-mischief, half-tenderness.

Tracy's answering smile faltered; her body stilled. He was magnificent. Like a fantasy come to life. Overwhelming in his size and power. She was crazy about him. She wanted him.

She was scared to death.

Nervous shivers swept over her body and she tried desperately to control them, to recapture her strength of purpose and sacrifice. She was going to help him. She was doing this to help him....

Help him? What the hell was she talking about? People didn't change in one evening. He'd wake up tomorrow, refreshed and relaxed, humming an I-got-laid-last-night melody and step back into his luxury life. While she'd go home and die an old maid's death in three days.

Paul pulled down his briefs and stepped out of them, stood before her, hands on his hips, studying her like a Greek god looking down on the mortals of the Earth, his erection jutting proudly.

Her shivers increased.

"Cold?" His eyebrows drew down.

She shook her head. And another thing. This guy had probably had every woman he wanted over the last decade or so. Hell, he could probably have any woman even if he *didn't* want her. What was he going to do when he encountered Miss too-small-boobs, not-very-experienced, had-trouble-reaching-climax Tracy? What made her think awarding herself to him like she was some valuable prize would do more than give him a so-so orgasm before he forgot her name? Did she think she had some magical powers over him no other woman had?

He slid onto the bed and lay next to her, put his hand on her shivery skin. "What's the matter?"

"I just...haven't done a lot of this." She stared woodenly at the ceiling, trying not to panic or cry.

"What, sex?"

"Sex...without feeling."

He turned her face toward him, frowning at what must be her expression of sheer virginal terror. "You don't have feelings for me?

"I...you said it would be like a thunderstorm." She raised her arm and gestured a cloudburst above her head. "Over, then done."

"I did, didn't I." He rolled away from her and clasped his hands behind his head, took in a long breath and let it out. "I think I was kidding myself."

Tracy's mouth dropped open. At the same time

lightness and hope started having a Mardi Gras parade through her body. Okay, so this didn't mean he was nuts over her. It could just mean he could see his way clear to doing her twice.

But it could mean more.

He looked at her cautiously. "What about you?"

"You mean do I have...feelings for you?" She shrugged, trying to seem invulnerable. *Only a truck-load.* "Oh...a few."

He grinned, turned back toward her on his side, his body looming over her, and slid his hand across her rib cage. "Nice feelings?"

"Very nice." Instead of a light tease, her voice came out a low, husky whisper, as if she were someone who'd barely survived a desert crossing.

His grin faded into intensity; he reached over and unbuttoned her shirt slowly with one skillful hand, unhooked the front of her bra, pushed the fabric aside and stroked her bare stomach. "Tell me what you want."

Tracy tensed at his murmured words and resisted the urge to cross her arms over her chest. Just like that? He wanted some kind of announcement? Lovemaking with her boyfriend in college had always been a silent, earnest affair. Now Paul wanted her to lie here and request items off the menu? Name her own body parts? "I...I don't—"

"Shhh. Okay." He kept up the stroking, sweeping her skin up and down again, each pass higher and each pass lower until his warm strong fingers brushed up under her breasts and down to the waistband of her jeans. The shivers stopped; she arched, hungry for a more intimate touch. Her legs parted, her hips made instinctive frustrated circles with nothing to push against. Then his hands were on her breasts, cupping, circling, rolling her nipples between his fingers with a roughness that made her whimper and say his name in an ecstatic whisper.

"Tell me what you want, Tracy."

"You know."

"Say it."

"No."

"Say it, Tracy. Please. I want to hear."

She swallowed. "...touch me."

"Where?"

"Between my...touch me."

He undid her jeans, pulled down the zipper, slid his hand inside, almost there, still not enough, making her tremble and strain for him. "Here?"

She arched so his hand plunged farther under her waistband, so his fingers touched the curling hair beneath her panties. Not enough. Not nearly enough. "Farther."

"Here?" He pushed in to cover her sex with his warm, wide palm.

"Yes." She kept her eyes shut, moved against him, breathless and crazy for him. "Yes."

"Now what?" His whisper was low against her temple, he drew a line with his lips down her cheek to the corner of her mouth.

She turned, kissed him ravenously, pushed her hips

against the hand that lay so infuriatingly still against her.

"Move." The word came out rough and desperate; she barely knew what she was saying, only that if he didn't touch her, move inside her she'd go completely out of her mind. "In me."

He let his breath out on a groan and slid his fingers up inside her, one, then two, entering her, then spreading her moisture out and around.

"Oh." She shook her head, arched away then came back against his hand. She was a starving demon, an animal. Driven by a need that made her gasp and pant and almost hurt.

He pulled his fingers out, found the center of her pleasure and rubbed, lightly at first, then harder, insistent.

"No." She'd come apart too soon. He should be with her. Hadn't she started out doing this for him? She pulled away. "Not like that."

"Yes." He followed her with his hand, touching until she knew he had to stop or it would be too late to control herself, too late to care. "I want to see you let go."

"No. I want you to...oh no." She clutched at his arm, tried to move his hand away. He resisted, kept the pace until she gave in, cried out and exploded into her climax, writhing against his fingers as the sensations went on and on, wave after wave, before they finally let her come down.

She went limp against him, damp with perspiration, still panting. "I thought I was doing this for you."

"Believe me, you were." He whispered the words

against her mouth and pulled her hard against him, his body tense, breath coming fast. He pushed her pants down and off, then her panties, and rolled her onto her back. "That was the sexiest thing I've ever seen."

He kissed her breasts, her stomach and down lower until the warm wetness of his tongue moved where his fingers had been.

Tracy shook her head even as her hips rose to meet the pressure. "It should be your turn."

He grinned up at her. "It will be. But I want you there with me again."

She lay back and let him taste her, unable to resist the sensation of slippery warmth. Incredibly, her desire rose again, slowly at first, then hot and insistent. She reached down and took hold of his arms, guided him up next to her. "Your turn *now*."

He laughed and reached into his nightstand for a condom, put it on and straddled her on his hands and knees. "If you say so."

She looked down at the length of him, hard and ready between his legs and opened hers to receive him, feeling happy and solemn and reluctant and impatient all at once.

"Tracy."

She looked up into his eyes, blue-gray and serious and tender.

"You're a pretty fabulous lady."

She caught her breath. "So are you."

He chuckled, then lowered his hips, keeping his torso up on his elbows, watching, guiding himself toward her. He found her center, then kept his body still and lifted his head to watch her. She felt herself drawn into his gaze, held there, anticipating their connection with almost unbearable intensity. Then he slid inside her, slowly, as if he were savoring every inch of their joining.

She closed her eyes.

"Look at me."

She tried, she tried. But the emotion was too much, the power generated by their merged bodies too much. She closed her eyes again. "I can't."

"Okay, okay," he whispered. "It's okay."

He pushed the rest of the way inside her and began to move. His strokes were slow and relaxed at first, his weight easy on top of her, arms encircling, cheek next to hers, their bodies rising and falling. Then his breathing sped, became uneven; he drew out farther, pushed in harder.

"Tracy." He kissed her—her neck, her cheek, her lips. His tongue slipped inside her mouth, kept pace with his thrusting body. Where there had been tenderness and sweetness there was now desperate passion, the overwhelming need to push toward and against him, to take him so far into her body that they melded into one individual. Pushing until her second release was only an inevitable climb up, a straining then effortless slide into the overwhelming sensation that made her cry out again, cling to him, contract helplessly around his still-thrusting hardness until he stopped, said her name and she felt him pulsing inside her.

That was it. Everything. The world. The cosmos. Alternate dimensions. Parallel universes. Everything she'd been searching for. Right here.

She drew her hands slowly up the smooth solid muscled skin of his back, blissful, breath slowing, relishing the feel of his sated weight on her, his nakedness pressed so close.

Okay. So it happened. She knew it could and now it had. He might have been kidding himself about the thunderstorm, might think she was a fabulous lady, but there was no question how Tracy felt. All her agony, all her searching for a place she belonged had come to an end in this one humbling fabulous moment.

She belonged with Paul Sanders.

10

"COME IN."

Tracy twisted the handle and walked into Allegra's apartment, sparsely furnished with a few sophisticated pieces in an overall Oriental flavor. A total contrast to the spirited Midwestern bundle of colors and jangly jewelry who inhabited it. Feng shui Allegra had called her latest adventure in decor. The arrangement of one's living space for optimum relaxation and mental health.

Whatever. If it worked, maybe Tracy should try it. Right now she was a serious emotional elevator, up to luxury penthouse ecstasy one minute, and plunging into smelly basement uncertainty the next.

"I'm just finishing." Allegra sat cross-legged, eyes closed, on a woven grass mat. She wore a shocking pink-and-yellow striped leotard with purple sweat-pants; her hair for once, was in its natural spiky-brown do.

Tracy flopped onto her black futon sofa and waited for her best friend from the U. of Wisconsin at Madison to finish achieving higher levels of spirituality or whatever she was doing. Since spending the night at Paul's had catapulted Tracy into the very highest level of sensuality, she could understand striving for higher things. The problem was getting herself to stay there.

Allegra's right eye peeked open, focussed on Tracy, then lowered again. "You slept with him."

"Huh?" Tracy stared. Allegra's powers of intuition were legendary; they'd called her Psychic Woman in college. "How did you know that?"

"Your aura is rosy and exudes satiation. Your eyes show happiness and womanly power." She stretched her arms up to the ceiling. "And your chin is all pink from his stubble."

"Oh." Tracy fingered the sensitive skin. "Yeah, that."

"You okay?" Allegra opened her eyes.

Tracy nodded, unable to contain either the goofy grin that spread over her face or the subsequent slide into nervous lip-biting.

"Aha." Allegra studied her curiously. "The Manhunters' first experiment leads to passion and uncertainty."

"That's about the size of it."

"You're in love with him." Allegra bounded to her feet, her short gymnast's body moving with athletic grace. "And not sure if he returns the feeling."

"...Yes." Tracy wove her fingers together. After what she and Paul shared last night, it seemed impossible that he didn't have strong feelings for her. But who knew with the male of the species? Not as if Tracy had loads of experience. And of course Paul hadn't thought to spell it all out and tape it to his forehead. "When I left his place this morning, we were both rushing to work, and all he said was that he'd call me."

"And he hasn't yet, even though it's been..." Allegra

glanced at her watch. "Only nine hours. Quit freaking."

Tracy got up from the couch. "I hate this. I hate not knowing how it will turn out. I hate not being in control of my own happiness. I hate feeling between things again. And most of all..." she took a deep breath, "I hate whining like this."

"Honey, welcome to love." Allegra chuckled. "It's a messy business."

"Last night when we...I mean after..." she rolled her eyes. "Being with him gave me this amazing sensation that I was all there for once. All in the present, not torn up and divided anymore. I can't really explain it."

"You just did." Allegra smiled and shrugged. "He makes you feel like a whole person. That's a happy thing."

"Then back at work today...it was like nothing had changed. I'm surrounded by paper and steel and wiring, shipments of fruit, shipments of vegetables, all represented by ink on paper. Dollars in and dollars out. What does that have to do with me? How I feel? Who I am?"

Allegra bent over and touched her toes, brought her torso to horizontal, then stood upright. "You know, too many people are ignoring their spiritual health on the job. Maybe I should incorporate that aspect into my seminars. Career mental health. Matching your job to your inner karma. Something like that." She tapped her chin and frowned. "Hmm, I'll think on it. Anyway, you want my advice?"

"Please." If anyone could tell her about making herself feel undivided it was Allegra.

"You feel ripped up right now. Paul makes you whole. But you can't control him wanting to be with you. So what do you do with your feelings? What else can you do to find peace? Where else can you go where you feel whole?"

Tracy grinned and whacked her forehead. "The farm."

"Exactly." Allegra bounded over and gave Tracy a hug. "Go up there tomorrow, spend the weekend finding yourself, a day or two to figure it out. I guarantee you'll find some answers there."

"Thanks." Tracy squeezed her friend close.

"But..." Allegra pulled back and looked earnestly into Tracy's face, her pretty eyes for once not obscured by clunky plastic frames. "Don't be surprised if the answers you get at the farm aren't the ones you're expecting."

"What do you mean?"

"You'll see." She gave a gentle smile.

Tracy made a frustrated growling noise. "I hate when you get all smug and mysterious."

Allegra laughed. "I know you do. And by the way, if you see any Manhunter prospects, send one my way, okay? I've been peering madly into men's eyes for a month now and nothing's happened. I have to find my dull-businessman-total-opposite so I can get rid of this 'kook' image and start pushing out the babies." She sighed. "But right now I'll get changed and we can go to dinner."

She disappeared into her bedroom. Tracy sank back onto the couch and hugged her arms around herself, grinning. Why hadn't she thought of going out to the farm? Just the thought of the cool, restful scenery and the warm, welcoming house made her feel calmer. She could sit out on the wraparound porch in a rocker and watch the sunset, make popcorn and eat the entire bowl watching old movies on TV. Crawl into bed surrounded by acres of growing green and feel safe and secure, at peace and...

She grimaced. Lonely.

There was no use denying it. After last night, after what she'd found with Paul, there'd be a hole in her life whenever he wasn't there. Even at the farm. She flopped back against the bright-red sofa pillows. Was love always this agonizing? Didn't some people get to slide blissfully into it? Well, not this woman. She had a lousy track record with life changes; they always spun her into confusion and anxiety. This change she really wanted to be for the better.

She suddenly sat bolt upright. *Hello?* Why was she moping around the obvious solution? Why couldn't Paul be at the farm with her? On the porch watching the sunset; sharing her popcorn in front of the movie; and oh yes, under the covers in her bed. Being there might give him some peace, too, connect him again with a simpler lifestyle, albeit not the type he'd grown up with.

That is...if he wanted to go with her. She sank back down. Guys freaked if they thought you were getting too serious too fast. A simple weekend invitation to them was like demanding a lifelong commitment. Maybe she'd be pushing it even to ask.

Come on, Tracy. She pushed herself up and off the couch. Time to stop being such a wimp. They were lovers now; she had every right to ask him to go away for a weekend.

She stopped. Except he said he'd call and he hadn't...

Enough! She put her hands to her head to stop the arguing. "Allegra, can I use your phone to check my messages before we go?"

Laughter came through Allegra's bedroom door. "Nine and a *half* hours and you snap?"

"I guess." Tracy rolled her eyes, dialed and punched in the code to retrieve her messages, heart pounding in anticipation.

Beep. "Tracy it's Paul."

She closed her eyes and drew in a long breath. *Thank you, thank you, thank you.*

"I wanted to call you earlier, but I never had more than a second. Let me know what you're doing this weekend. I'd like to get together. Call me. I'm at the office, heading home around seven."

The machine beeped off.

Tracy stared at the wall until the beep stopped registering in her brain, then launched full tilt into The Undignified Dance of the Very Very Joyous around Allegra's apartment, laughing breathlessly. She was going to the farm this weekend, to find herself, to reestablish contact with who she really was. In the process she could do more to help Paul allow his past back into his own life. A whole weekend back home where she belonged, just the way she'd envisioned. Safe and secure and at peace.

But now definitely not lonely.

PAUL BLEW OUT his breath in a sigh that lifted the edges of the paperwork spread on his kitchen table and sent one sheet sailing off onto the floor. He didn't bother to retrieve it.

She wanted to go away for the weekend to her family's farm.

Aside from that one fabulous night with Tracy, his week had been hell. The 21st Century campaign was going nowhere fast. Ideas came and went; he and his team pounced on some, followed up with others until the dead end hit, but nothing had leaped out as the obvious choice. For the first time in his career, he was starting to panic. The idea was out there, the perfect one, but they had their first presentation to Tracy's father in a week, and he had yet to snag it.

Now Tracy wanted to spend the weekend at the farm. He'd put off deciding, telling her he needed to see how much work he could get done tonight and tomorrow. True. But he already knew the answer he wanted to give. He needed to be hooked electronically, needed to keep working, needed his equipment. She'd be a total obsessive distraction. No way could he work there.

He leaned back and clasped his hands behind his head. If he could just come up with a hook—a slogan, or a new name for the product, the accompanying images would fall into place. But ascribing sizzle and charm to a tomato was straining even his talents.

Of course he could face the reality that the quiet atmosphere at the farm might jog his creativity in new and unexpectedly fruitful directions.

Or he could face the fact that, simply put, he dreaded going.

Peel and eat, nice and neat. No seeds, no sweat.

Ugh.

It wasn't Tracy he was avoiding. God, no. After that incredible taste of what they could be like together, he was ravenous for her. Not just her body, either; her smile, the way her eyes lit up when she let herself go, the way she seemed so blissfully unaware of her remarkable qualities. Her hidden sensuality, her passions, her ideals. He respected her immensely; he wanted her desperately; he could even imagine falling in love with her.

But then there was that damn farm.

He really should go. No point dragging out their relationship without confronting this gigantic hurdle. The earlier the better, really. Before he got in too deep, fell too hard, and cut himself to shreds backing out.

Hot tomatoes for cool customers. Saucy Red.

Ugh.

The problem was the way she felt about that place—like God had created it on the eighth day. Plus the fact that her invitation felt very much like some kind of test she expected him to pass with flying colors, and he wasn't sure he would.

He'd seen his own apartment through her eyes for

the first time when they'd come back from Nate's. Safe to say, he'd gone a little overboard making sure he and everyone else knew he'd made it or was well on his way. But he wasn't convinced she could see her farm with the same objective eyes she'd made possible for him. Not that it wouldn't be charming as farmhouses went. Wonderful even. A place they could have a fabulous romantic weekend escape.

But someone like Tracy could enjoy so much more, should open herself up to the new world of experiences she was lucky enough to have available to her. It was as snobbish and stale of her to insist on worshipping all things plebeian as it was for him to have filled his apartment with only the best.

Treat the cook in your life. Get out of the kitchen, get on with your dreams.

Ugh.

His suit felt suddenly stiff and confining. He got up and went into his bedroom, pulling off his tie. Those jeans had felt pretty great the other night. Easy and familiar, like friends he hadn't seen in a while but could take up with right where they'd left off. He rooted through his bottom drawer, came up with a pair of cutoffs he hadn't worn in years and pulled them on. They felt damn good too. He grinned and rummaged farther in the drawer. His Harley-Davidson T-shirt from a biker who'd given him a ride as a motorcycle-worshipping teenager. A Red Sox baseball cap he'd hung over the dugout at Fenway to get Carl Yastrzemski to sign. He'd been a fool to bury these memories away.

Time to dig up and replant. Time to put his money and experience to better use than designer labels and finding ways to seduce people out of their money. Wasn't there some mentor program he could join? Big Brother, maybe. Give back some of what he'd achieved and make a difference in some kid's life.

Idealistic sure, but he hadn't had an idealistic thought in a long time and it felt damn good.

He took out the cap, brought it into the living room and looked around. On the fireplace mantel, center stage, was a little marble sculpture of...something or other, that Paul thought of as "The Blob" the first time he saw it, then stopped looking. He picked it up and stuck it behind his Bose speakers, then arranged the hat so the signed brim tilted up against the wall.

Looked like crap. But it made the exact kind of statement he was in the mood to make, so it stayed.

He laughed out loud, crossed to his CD player, put in Oscar Peterson at full blast, boogied into the kitchen and got out a plastic garbage bag. Time for Paul's Rampage.

The low arrangement of dried plants and twisty gnarled sticks. *Outta here.* The coffee table volume of *Scenic Walks in Provence. Outta here.* The Tiffany paperweight; the painting of six brightly colored squares; the brass kidney-shaped bowl designed by some famous artist's not-as-talented offspring. *Outta here.*

Half an hour later he surveyed the results proudly. Still in good taste, but it looked more like a place he'd want to live now, and less like some decorator's idea of decorated. Maybe he could buy some posters or prints or new art to fill up the walls. Maybe Tracy would like to help him pick them out.

He sighed and went back into the kitchen, dropped the garbage bag with a clank and made a note to donate the stuff somewhere. He liked the idea of doing something fun and domestic with Tracy. He liked it a lot. But until she'd worked through her hang-ups about money, he didn't see the domestic stuff lasting until death did them part.

He sat back down and stared dismally at his notes.

Terrific Tomatoes. Peel-easy players.

What's good for the sauce can be good to the cook.

Never put off until tomato...

Ugh.

A picture of Tracy lying on his bed came into his head for only the six- or seven-thousandth time that week. She was watching him undress, waiting for him to slide inside her, closing her eyes against the emotion he knew they were both feeling. Her face was so clear and readable, her eyes so expressive when they lost their deadening coat of sadness.

She was worth fighting for.

A new burst of energy shot through him. If he could come this far under her influence, begin to make peace with his past by bringing it into his present, maybe he could do the same for her, on a deeper level than making sure she liked foie gras. And what better place to start than by taking on the blasted farm?

The farm. An image jumped into his head with a certainty that made him breathless. He grabbed a pen, tore off a scribbled-on sheet of paper from his pad and started to write on the exposed clean sheet. *Perfect. Perfect.* Capturing the essence of the product and the appeal of the family business. *Perfect.*

He jumped up from the table and ran to the phone to call Karen and Jim, adrenaline sparking him into action. Starting tomorrow they'd go into overdrive, get this thing in shape in time for the campaign pitch and blow Derek Richards's socks off.

He dialed Jim's number and pumped his fist in the air. He had it now.

"Jim, it's Paul. I got it."

"Hey, all right." Jim's voice brightened with anticipation. "Let me hear."

"Short, simple, to the point. You ready?"

"Hell, yeah."

Paul grinned. He had a campaign, and with any luck he'd have a serious shot at happy ever after as well.

"I'm calling them...Tracy's Tomatoes."

11

"TURN HERE." Tracy pointed to Lavaham's Lane, nearly bursting with excitement when the headlights of Paul's Lexus picked up the anticipated rectangular green glow of the street sign. The farm and Paul. She couldn't think of anything better in the entire universe except maybe if her mom were still alive. But since even the power of love couldn't bring Mom back, Tracy would settle for using that power on the man driving beside her.

It had seemed almost obscene to bring a Lexus out to Oak Ridge. Paul insisted he drive, though, and she had to admit that in the horrendous August heat and humidity, the car had been air-conditioned, leather-upholstered, smooth-riding heaven. Happily, now that night had fallen, the air would cool and a breeze would start whispering through the fields.

"There!" She gestured ahead. "Turn here, the house is at the end of the drive."

The Lexus bumped and jarred over the rutted lane. The ghostly neat rows of tassled corn showed gray in the moonlight, green in the headlights. Ever since her family had gone into business, her dad only maintained a few acres for experimental plants and his greenhouses. But he couldn't bear to part with the land that had supported and nurtured them for so many years, land he and her mother had put so much into. So he rented out the fields, to keep the rich soil producing life-sustaining crops.

She glanced over at Paul. Not that she expected him to match her level of excitement at seeing an old farmhouse, but he'd been awfully quiet in the last half hour of the trip, since they'd left the highway. Maybe he was tired from his week and the long drive. Maybe he was preoccupied with the 21st Century campaign. Or maybe he was drawn, as she always was, to the restful rolling landscape, the sense of space and freedom. Maybe it resonated through him the same way it did through her, only now she could add in pride and deep happiness at being able to share it with him.

"There it is!" The familiar welcoming structure rose black against the moonlit sky and she laughed from the sheer joy of that first sighting. Paul slowed the car to a stop in front of the old garage and she tumbled out into the clean, warm night air, the chirp of crickets and rustle of corn, and raced over to the front porch. "Hello, House!"

She turned back to the car and laughed again at her own over-the-top enthusiasm, at the smell of earth, mature plants and summer-evening sweetness.

Paul got out of the car slowly, keeping his headlights on, and grinned at her, hands on his hips, looking sexy, slightly rumpled and slightly awkward and out of place even in jeans and a casual shirt. "You talk to your house?"

She danced toward him, feet crunching the gravel

path and threw her arms around his neck. He'd blend into his surroundings in no time. He needed a chance to adjust. "Yes, I talk to my house. I'm a total case. Come on, let's unload and I'll show you around."

She planted a kiss on his mouth and raced to her side of the car, grabbed her tiny battered suitcase and one of the bags of groceries they'd stopped for on the way, then watched impatiently as Paul pulled out his overnight case and laptop, hefted the other bag from the supermarket, turned off the headlights and locked the car.

Tracy gestured him up the path to the front steps of the house, frowning. Mr. Laptop might have to be kidnapped and buried in the garden in the dead of night. She wanted Paul all to herself this weekend. Greedy, maybe, but that's the selfish kind of chick she was right now. Besides, the farm wasn't the place to think about any form of capitalism. Advertising, marketing, profits, sales—they didn't belong here.

But she sure as hell did. And she'd bet her bottom dollar by the end of the weekend Paul would, too.

They climbed the front steps and walked through the screen door of the porch up to the front entrance. Tracy fumbled for her keys and fit the proper one into the lock, hands trembling with anticipation.

The lock stuck as it always did; Tracy shoved with her shoulder and turned the bolt the rest of the way. The door gave way suddenly and swung into the house, revealing the worn plank flooring of the entranceway and the rag rug her mom had made.

"Here we are." She walked into the still-sweltering

stuffy stillness. Breathing the familiar scent rapturously, she led the way to the kitchen, down the short hallway hung with family photos in homemade frames. "We'll have to open windows to let in the fresh air."

"There's no air-conditioning?"

Tracy laughed, hoping she'd imagined the note of dismay in his voice. He'd see. Once the windows were open the house would cool quickly. "Nope. We absolutely *live* out on the porch in the summer. We even sleep out there. We'll do that tonight."

"Oh." He put his groceries on the counter.

Tracy took the laptop and bag out of his other arm, put them down and wrapped herself around him. "You'll love it, City Boy, I promise. There are even beds out there. We can push two together and have ourselves a king."

"Now you're talking." He chuckled and she lifted her face and kissed his firm sexy mouth until his body tensed and he pulled her close against him. "Why don't you show me those beds now?"

She batted her eyelashes with exaggerated innocence. "Don't you want to see the rest of the house?"

"Of *course* I want to see the house, but won't it be that much more spectacular in the morning light?" His hands slid down her hips to rock her against him.

"Mmm. You do have a point." Tracy closed her eyes. Heat was already spreading through her body and they hadn't even gotten naked yet. The man had turned her into a ravenous harlot. "Let's put the groceries away, fast."

They rummaged hurriedly through the bags for perishable items and put them away in the old, loudly humming refrigerator.

Tracy held up a box that must have slid by her at the supermarket. "*Microwave* popcorn?"

He blinked. "No microwave?"

She shook her head. "We make popcorn on the stove."

"I can live with that."

"Good." She tossed the box back into the bag and gave him a come-hither look. "I think that's everything."

He grinned and took her hand. She led him outside into the welcoming coolness of the porch and around to the north side of the house where the beds stayed out all year, always left with clean linens by the last user. "Here."

They took off the protective plastic covers, pulled back the nearly threadbare spreads and slid impatiently onto the worn-soft sheets.

"Now this," Paul stretched out next to her on his side and stroked up under her shirt across her rib cage, "is farm living at its finest."

Tracy laughed and reached her arms up over her head, let him pull off her shirt and unhook her bra, her body thrumming in anticipation, her heart singing a similar tune. Paul here at the farm. She couldn't get over how perfect it was. How complete.

He kissed her mouth, her neck, down her shoulder and pulled back. Tracy held her breath, then arched up with a soft cry when his mouth found her breast in the moonlit darkness, when his warm tongue circled her nipple, circled then pulled in quick bursts of suckling.

He was making her hot, crazy, making her body feel sexy and worshipped. She'd climax easily again with him, and end up feeling sated, loved, spent.

She wanted to do that for him.

"Paul." She gently moved his head from her breast.

"You don't like that?"

She laughed. "Um. No, that's not exactly it."

"What, then." He moved up next to her, kissed her temple, her cheek, slid his hand down and unbuttoned her shorts, his breathing slow and heavy.

She aroused him. He would get pleasure from their lovemaking, no question. But she wanted more; she wanted to show him the kind of woman she could be. The kind of woman she was here at her family's house. Confident, in control. So happy.

And frankly, she wouldn't mind seeing him go completely out of his mind with pleasure, either. He'd already gotten that opportunity *twice* with her.

She stopped his hand burrowing under the waistband of her shorts. "Let me."

"Let you what?"

"Do what you were going to do."

"You're going to touch yourself?" His voice came out in an awed and slightly hopeful whisper.

She hadn't been planning to. She was just going to undress herself in front of him. But..."Would you like me to?"

"Oh, Tracy."

His voice said it all, deep and husky and practically

grateful, producing an immediate rush of excitement, a thrilling vision of her female potential.

She got up onto her knees; he lay back, his features silver in the moonlight spilling onto the bed.

She'd never taken the lead like this. But for some reason she had every confidence she could; every confidence that she could bring him to the brink of yelling out his frustration and eagerness for her and for his release. She'd never felt anything like this potency, this sense of herself as a sexual being. As if something inside her that had only been peeking at freedom before suddenly found the strength to bend back the bars of whatever cage it had been hiding in and bust loose.

This house, this farm was so good for her. Why had she ever left?

"Watch me," she whispered, and spread her knees so her shorts stayed trapped halfway down her thighs, so the zipper parted and strained, so her panties were visible in the vee opening.

She stroked her stomach, drew her hands up to cup her own breasts, then slid them down again just to the top of her panties. "Are you watching?"

"Yes." His voice came out hoarse and breathless in the semidarkness. "I'm watching."

Her fingers slid across the top of the elastic, then dipped under until she felt her own curls, her own moisture.

His breath shot in and rushed out on a brief moan. "I can't see. Show me."

She pushed her knees together until her shorts fell to the bed, then slid her panties down so her sex was exposed to the cool night air coming in through the screen, so the glint of moonlight shone on the curling hair between her legs.

And she touched herself. Lightly at first, hesitantly, then bolder and more directly as she relaxed, and allowed herself the pleasure it brought, rolling her head, undulating her body, watching Paul's increasing torture with a strange combination of tenderness and fierce satisfaction.

"I can't take this." He sat up and began unbuttoning his shirt.

"Let me." She shed her shorts and panties, as impatient for him as he was for her, pushed him back on the bed, undid his shirt and helped him pull it off. She felt alight, alive, beyond aroused. Powerful and free. She unbuttoned and unzipped his jeans, put her face to the vee and pressed her cheek against the hot bulging cotton of his briefs.

"Tracy, you're going to kill me."

She smiled and kissed up the length of his erection, reaching around his hips to lower his jeans. He was ready, waiting, straining with anticipation. She made him wait, kissing lightly, teasing with flicks of her tongue before she brought him into her mouth firmly, enhancing the rhythm with her fingers, letting her body join in the motion.

One minute, maybe two and he reached down, hauled her up beside him and fumbled in his jeans for a condom. Thirty seconds and he was ready, pulling her down. She resisted.

"This is my show." She pushed him back on the bed

and straddled him, lifted and took him inside her, gasping at the contact, at the sheer potency of their joining. The night air caressed them as she rocked over him, slowly, letting them both savor the rhythm and the pressure.

She wanted their lovemaking to show how right they were together here, how deeply she wanted to share this bond and this place with him forever. Out here on the porch she'd slept in every summer of her life, where she'd been read to by her parents, lost her first tooth, had her first kiss. Now she could add more memories, sexy grown-up woman memories, to this place that had so cherished her.

He lifted his hips into her, slid his hands up her thighs and increased her pleasure with his fingers until she felt the inevitable pull begin. She rocked faster and gave herself over, to him, to her climax, dimly aware in the burst of sensations that he'd grabbed her hips and thrust hard up into her until he echoed her sounds of pleasure.

She slumped down onto Paul's warm, welcoming chest; he clasped her against him, their bodies still pulsing occasionally as they came down into peace. And love. Lord, she loved him.

Here at the farm with Paul in her arms and in her body, she had everything she'd ever wanted.

TRACY GRADUALLY came to consciousness, warm and deliciously relaxed, aware of the sun already up and heating the morning air. She burrowed closer to the male body next to her, frowned, and lifted her head.

Paul was staring up at the ceiling. When she moved, he turned stiffly and smiled. "Sleep well?"

"Like a log. You?"

He grimaced. "Not quite a log. Maybe a twig."

She struggled up onto her elbows. "Weren't you comfortable?"

"Yes, I was comfortable. And so were approximately twenty mosquitoes, two flies and that." He pointed to the corner of the porch.

Tracy sat up and caught sight of a rabbit just disappearing through a sizeable hole in the screen.

"I think he was doing the bunny hop all night with his pals." He sounded distinctly grumpy.

She leaned over and kissed his chest and cheek, wincing at the red marks of mosquito bites on his neck and shoulders. "I'll get us some breakfast. About a gallon of coffee okay?"

"That'll do for a start." He yawned and tousled her curls, pulled her down on top of him and ran his hands over her body. "*You'll* do for a start."

Forty-five minutes later, Tracy stumbled into the kitchen, flushed and smiling. She opened the refrigerator and pulled out breakfast items, wondering if life could possibly get any better.

"Mmm. Bacon and eggs." Paul came into the kitchen and put his arms around her, cradling her against his body, rocking her back and forth. "Mind if I shower first?"

"Bathe."

"Bathe? Is that farm talk for shower?"

"We don't have a shower. You have to take a bath."

He stopped rocking. "A bath."

She twisted in his arms and smiled up at his incredulous face. "You know, stop the drain, run the water, get in and wash..."

He squeezed her and let go. "I just haven't taken one since I was a kid."

"Very relaxing. And don't be surprised at the noise the hot water pipes make. Sort of a screech and then some banging. And the water will probably be brown at first, so let it run for a while."

"Okay. Screech. Bang. Brown water. Sounds terrific."

Tracy laughed. "You'll love it."

She arranged plates and utensils on a tray and set the old wooden picnic table out on the porch, giggling when horrendous noises announced that Paul had started his bath. He was probably freaking even though she'd warned him.

Back in the kitchen, she laid the strips of bacon in an iron pan and turned on the stove to get it started heating. The house definitely had its own eccentric personality, like a cherished, slightly senile great-grandmother who'd been alive forever and everyone adored. Paul would get used to it.

The bacon started spitting; she turned the heat down, put in the toast, set the oven timer, since the toaster had long since stopped popping the toast at the appropriate time, and on impulse ran outside to cut some daisies for the table from the garden her mom had planted so many years ago now. She lingered for a short while among the flowers, absorbing the fresh early morning scent, lifting her face to the pure country sunshine.

Nowhere did she feel so content, so whole, so at peace with who she was. There was nothing like it anywhere else in the world. And it was hers.

The toast. Clutching the daisies, she raced back into the house and saw Paul, naked and wet, barreling into the kitchen at the same time she registered the hoarse croaking scream of the kitchen timer and the smell of burning.

Damn.

She rushed in after him, threw the daisies on a counter.

"Ow!" Paul jerked his hand back from the smoking toaster. "How do you get the toast to pop up?" He had to shout over the screech of the timer.

"Unplug it," she shouted back, and headed for the timer, wrestling with it for several seconds before she managed to turn it off.

"The bacon." She sprang to the stove, grabbed the handle and yelled.

Paul lunged toward her, shoved her hand under the faucet, turned on cold water and grabbed a kitchen towel to protect his own hands. He took the pan off the stove, turned the strips of bacon, which only had a few blackened spots, put the pan back on the stove and took a deep, deep breath.

"Tracy."

"Yes?" Tracy examined the red stripe on her hand and put it back under the water.

"Why don't you have a pan with a safety handle?"

"Well, I don't know. We've had this one forever. Iron is an excellent—"

"How long have you had that toaster?"

"Gosh, I don't know. Forever, too, I suppose."

"It doesn't pop the toast up on its own?"

"No. That's why I set the timer. But I should tell you, in case you ever need to do the same, that you have to set this timer two minutes longer than you want, because—"

"Tracy." He came forward and gripped her shoulders. "May I ask the obvious question?"

She frowned. "What's the obvious question?"

"If your toaster and your timer don't work, why don't you buy new ones?"

"They work fine." She shrugged. What was he getting so upset about? "If I hadn't left to cut flowers we would have had perfect toast."

"Okay." He nodded, though she had a feeling he was far from accepting her answer. "Okay. I'm going to get dressed."

"Great. Though I like you fine in the raw." She smiled and got on her tiptoes for a kiss, pressing her body against his. Maybe he woke up cranky every morning. A lot of people did. She could live with that.

She scrambled the eggs and scraped the burned parts off the toast, managed to get the second side of the bacon perfect, put the daisies in a vase and carried everything out onto the porch.

Paul found her a minute later and they sat and ate, crunching loudly on the salvaged toast. A breeze brought them summer morning scents through the screen; butterflies darted among the flowers in the garden; birds chatted and argued overhead in the oak tree nearest the house.

Tracy finished and pushed back her plate, stretched her legs carefully along the bench so as not to get splinters, and leaned her chin on her hands, staring dreamily out at the fields of corn in the distance.

"Isn't this fabulous?"

"It's really great, Tracy." He shifted a few times as if he couldn't quite get comfortable, and winced.

"Splinter?"

He sighed, reached down and came up with a tiny sliver of wood. "Yup."

"Sorry. We've had this bench—"

"Forever, I know." He smiled and touched her cheek, but something stayed serious in his eyes. "So what were you planning to do this morning?"

"I'm planning to sit out on this porch all morning and do nothing."

"Sounds perfect." He stood and moved carefully away from the bench. "I'll get my laptop."

"Your laptop." Her stomach sank. High-tech was obscenely out of place in this idyllic, natural, old-as-the-hills setting, especially on their first weekend away together. Couldn't he see that?

"What." He stopped on his way into the house, hands on his hips. "You don't want me to work?"

"I thought...we could just sit together and watch the morning."

"Oh." He nodded as if he was trying to show that watching the morning had been a close second on his list of things to do. "Well, that sounds terrific. So I'll just sit here—" He plunked his large body into the porch swing before she could warn him about the fraying rope. "—and watch."

He said the last word from the floor. He did not sound happy. Tracy rushed over and helped him up. "I'm sorry. The second I saw you headed there I started to warn you, but it was too late."

"It's okay." Paul dusted himself off with sharp, jerky movements. "You know, I'm not really a sit-and-watch- the-morning kind of guy, Tracy. But I would really love to get to a fax machine. So if you could give me directions, I will go there and fax what I need to fax and *you* can sit and watch the morning. Okay?"

She nodded and gave him directions. She didn't blame him for being annoyed. Mosquitoes, burned toast, splinters and crashing to the floor didn't really put you in the mindset to sit and watch the morning. But she could do that while he was gone.

Except the minute Paul left, she had about zero interest in the morning. A strange restlessness invaded her. Almost as if she'd rather have gone with him, on dusty bumpy roads, to some crowded cement and steel building.

As if.

She went into the kitchen, wrinkled her nose at the burned smell and struggled for five minutes trying to open the window. Damn thing always stuck in the summer. She gave up, turned on the kitchen fan instead and started washing up, scrubbing the stuck bacon off the iron pan. Great. Now it would probably have to be reseasoned—oiled then heated in the oven, which needed careful watching since it didn't maintain a constant temperature.

In very little time, her do-nothing morning had changed into a work-hard morning. Seemed everywhere she looked something needed mending or cleaning. She really needed to spend more time here, to keep the place in shape. Strangely, her mood had also changed from cheerful and relaxed, to crabby and tense.

At the sound of Paul's car, her heart leaped back up into "happy" territory. She threw down her scrubbing brush and ran outside to greet him. He was just pulling a huge bag out of his back seat.

"What's this?" She lifted her face for a kiss and stared at the bag.

"I'll show you." He swung the bag over his shoulder like Santa Claus, brought it into the house and crouched next to it.

"This..." He grinned mysteriously and pulled out a box. "...is a toaster. It runs on a computer chip that senses the moisture level in the bread and when it's done exactly right, guess what? It pops it up."

"Paul..." Her stomach sank. He didn't get it. He didn't understand the magic of the farm.

"This..." he pulled out a colorful plastic item. "...is a kitchen timer. The amazing thing about this kitchen timer is that whatever number of minutes you set it to, that's how many it counts off!"

"Paul, I don't think—"

"The non-hand-searing cookware." He brought out a stack of different-sized, nonstick pans. "For my popcorn, a microwave. And coming this afternoon, a window unit air conditioner, because if it's all the same to you, I would rather not sleep out in the jungle again."

She shook her head, an eerie buzzing in her ears, her breath high and shallow. "I can't believe you got all this stuff."

"Why?" He gave her a strange look. As if he already knew, but wanted to hear it from her.

"Because this house is—"

"A museum."

"*What?*"

"It's a museum, Tracy. A shrine to deprivation. I have news for you—deprivation is not worthy of worship."

She stared at him incredulously. This was ten times worse than she thought. To him everything was about ease and luxury and comfort. About throwing money at whatever bothered you to make it go away. "How can you say that, knowing how special this place is to me?"

"Because it's true. You glorify things that are uncomfortable and inconvenient for absolutely no reason except that it comfortably and conveniently means you don't have to accept your new life or actually live it."

She cringed away from him. How could he have pretended all this time that things were wonderful between them when he was thinking all those horrible hurtful things about her? "You think I'm *scared* of living?"

"Yes." He got up from his crouch and took her shoulders. "I do. Because I see it in your eyes all the time, the sadness and the fear."

"No, you don't understand. That sadness is because I was taken out of the life I loved and pushed against my will into this new one. I don't fit the new one, Paul. I was happy when I lived here. I'm not happy now."

"You aren't *letting* yourself be happy."

Tracy squelched a shout of aggravation. This again? Didn't anyone understand? What was it about her devotion to the farm that threatened people? "Spare me the melodrama! You sound just like my friends."

"Didn't you say friends can have a better perspective on yourself than you do? Well, they're right." He made a huge gesture of frustration. "It's like you're determined *not* to be happy. You close yourself off to new experiences, don't even realize how lucky you are to have them available to you. You spend all your time pining for something that's gone."

She bristled, tried to swallow. Her face felt pinched, as if her skin had shrunk. "The house isn't gone."

"No." He sighed. "But the life you lived here is."

She stared at him, pushing back the panic and the angry tears threatening to spring into her eyes. She wasn't going to show him how much he hurt her. "You hate it here because there isn't a designer label on everything."

"Tracy, I don't hate it here." He put his hands to his temples and let them drop so they slapped against his thighs. "I just want to be comfortable."

"Oh? What's next on your list of comfortable, a swimming pool and Jacuzzi? Sauna and weight room?" She threw open her arms, anger and hurt making her lash out before she had a chance to process what she was saying. "Better yet, raze the damn albatross and build something with three stories and ten bedrooms, television in every room, wet bars and—"

"Shut up, Tracy. That's not what I meant."

"I think it is." Her voice shook; she folded her arms across her chest to keep them from shaking, too. "You're the one who's scared. You're so scared of your own past you wouldn't even eat a freaking hamburger."

"You're right." He nodded, his voice gentler now. "I was. You helped me see that, and I am genuinely and humbly grateful to you and I always will be. But what is really crucial for you and I if we're going to be together, and what I'm not getting from you now, is that you're trying to come to terms with changes in your life, too."

She gritted her teeth. He was talking to her as if she were a stupid child who had no grasp of the world outside. "I *have* come to terms with my new life. Rejecting certain aspects was a conscious decision, not some kind of denial."

"Don't shut me out, Tracy." His voice grew softer, more gentle, as if the angrier and more hysterical she got, the more damn controlled and sweet he became. "Try to hear what I'm saying."

"I hear you. Loud and clear. My family's house isn't good enough for your exalted taste, and no matter how much I love it the way it is, it therefore needs changing. Apparently the same applies to me. Well, you can call off your air-conditioning invasion because I'm sleeping on the porch tonight. If you don't want to join me you are free to go back to Milwaukee and enjoy the rest of your weekend in air-conditioned, pampered, utterly soulless comfort. I can take a bus back to the city when I'm ready to face it."

Her body trembled, her voice came out high and thin; she had a surreal feeling that this wasn't really happening, that she hadn't really said what she'd said, that the ugly moods and words would vanish into the peace and sunshine reality of the house and garden like the unpleasant mirage they were.

Except they didn't.

Instead, Paul narrowed his eyes. "That's what you want?"

She swallowed, anger rushing out of her and leaving dismal weariness in its place. "No. But I don't see any alternative."

"That's what I mean." He stepped closer and looked at her with such noble sadness in his eyes she wanted to slug him. "Your life is so full of alternatives, waiting to be explored, and you're not letting yourself see any of them. You want me to go? I'll go. But it's a waste. A damn waste."

He went back into the house, probably to retrieve his things. To leave. Tracy gave in to one sob, one set of tears and clenched the rest back. Why couldn't she have fallen in love with someone easy and natural and comfortable wherever he went? Someone who'd accept her, not try to change her? Someone who'd recognize the farm's quirky beauty for what it was, and love it at first sight, with the same passion she did?

Paul came back out onto the porch, holding his laptop and stuffing a few last toiletries into his bag.

"What we have is too good to let go this easily, Tracy." He leaned forward and kissed her fiercely. "You have my number. Call me when you're ready."

"Ready to be what *you* want me to be?"

"Ready to accept that your life has changed. Ready to change with it."

He banged through the porch screen and down the

steps, strode to his car and hurled his bag into the back seat.

She wrapped her arms around herself, frustration rising and sticking in her throat. This couldn't be happening. Not when everything was supposed to be so perfect this weekend. Instead of accepting and learning, he'd taken her and her beautiful house on as if they were renovation projects that needed to be upgraded.

Well, maybe it was just as well he was leaving. How far could they go together when their needs were so different? They'd fight and debate from the moment they woke up to the moment they went to bed. Great sex wasn't enough. Love wasn't even enough.

The Lexus motor started, revved. Paul turned the car around, stopped, and opened his window. "Tracy."

She walked to the edge of the porch and peered dully through the screen. "Yes?"

"Don't take the bus back to Milwaukee. Rent a car. A luxury one." He waved and started slowly down the driveway, leaning out the window with a sudden mischievous grin. "I dare you."

12

TRACY PULLED HERSELF up off the porch swing, newly mended with strong nylon rope. After an initial day of moping and feeling sorry for herself, she'd thrown herself into home improvement projects—sweeping, polishing, sanding and mending. But though she'd made the house look fresh and lived in, the work didn't seem to banish this strange restlessness. A restlessness she'd never felt here before.

The sun was just setting, turning clouds orange and pink, and fading away the deep blue of the sky at the horizon. She didn't seem to be in the mood to watch the sunset tonight. She didn't seem to be in the mood to do much of anything. Five days without Paul, five days without human contact. Solitude usually suited her fine when she was out here. But apparently since she'd met Paul, what was "usual" would have to be redefined.

She had called her father once, to let him know she'd be out of the office this week. He'd been fine with her absence professionally, but was obviously worried personally. He'd really wanted things to work out between her and Paul. To the point where he'd apparently invented the Great Guacamole Disaster of

Guajolote, Texas, with Becky's help, to get Tracy and Paul alone for lunch at Chez Mathilde.

Well, she wanted things to work out with Paul, too. But wanting wasn't enough.

She shuffled into the house, used the bathroom and scowled at herself in the mirror while she washed her hands. Hair a chaotic wreck; makeup cancelled due to lack of interest. Dark circles from fitful sleep interrupted by strange dreams. Dreams that the house had been turned into a giant pink golf resort by a developer who looked suspiciously like Paul. Dreams that she'd wandered onto a construction site and stepped in quick-drying cement where she stuck, flailing her arms, trying vainly to shout for help, while the rest of the world went on unconcernedly around her.

But worst by far, were the dreams of making love with Paul, of the fabulous, joyous feeling of completion, of the terrible fear she'd never feel that way again. Those dreams were the worst, because those dreams played in a continuous loop during the day, when she was fully awake and there was no escape.

She dragged herself into the family room and flicked on the old television, adjusting the antenna until the picture came in clearly. A movie starring Mel Gibson. God, how bad must she have it if even *he* paled in comparison to Paul? She sank onto the beat-up sofa, still decorated with a few hairs from Tinker, their dog who died shortly after Tracy's mom. No amount of vacuuming seemed to be able to clear them all away. No amount of busy work or wishing seemed to be able to clear the confusion from her brain.

A close-up of Mel's mesmerizing blue eyes refocussed Tracy's attention to his character's plight. She frowned when he lost his beautiful soul mate to an accident that left her in a coma. She shook her head when he was frozen by his scientist best friend and accidentally revived fifty years later. She smiled in sympathy as he tried to find his way around a totally changed world. That, she could certainly identify with.

The movie broke for a commercial and Tracy wandered into the kitchen to make popcorn since cooking dinner held no appeal. She measured oil into a pot, added a few tablespoons of kernels, and turned on the stove. A horrible buzz sounded, like an enormous electric shock. Sparks stuttered out of the burner coil and a blue-orange flame licked greedily at the pot.

Tracy yelled and flung herself away, then reached and shut off the stove, snatching her hand back as if it might get eaten. She stood, panting, fist to her chest, trying to get control of her breathing. The second her heart began to slow, she started crying. Ugly, wracking sobs that made her want to laugh because they were so melodramatic and unlike her, except she was too miserable to laugh. The counter hit her back and she slid down onto the floor and cried some more.

In her beautiful wonderful perfect sheltered little world, she was no longer happy. No longer complete. She might as well be in a giant deep freeze along with Mel. Fifty years could disappear and she'd still be here, watching TV, wrestling with the stove and the toaster and the windows. Tracy Richards, that weird old woman who lived by herself in the drafty ramshackle farmhouse. Kids would be scared to come by on Halloween and would dare each other to throw stones through her window. She'd hobble out on her cane, gray hair to her waist, most of her teeth missing, and shake her broomstick at them.

Tracy's tears changed to hysterical giggles. *Okay, enough.* Her life wouldn't come to that. She wouldn't let it. Maybe she'd spent the past few years treading water, but she wasn't going to stay in and get pruny skin anymore. Time to start swimming forward, find a nice island with room for two people in love, a nice house and plenty of compromises. She pushed herself up and grabbed a tissue, blew her nose, wiped her eyes and extended her arms sharply as if she needed to shoot her hands out of too-long sleeves.

Toaster first.

She pulled the plug out of the wall, rummaged under the sink for a large sturdy trash bag, and dumped it in. Kitchen timer next. Burned potholders, dull can opener, chipped glasses, cracked plates. This. Felt. Good.

Ugly wall clock, greasy teakettle, stained dishrack, threadbare towels, bent forks, rusted spatula. She laughed, positive adrenaline running for the first time all week. Mismatched mugs, shelf paper with red chickens, faded decades-old curtains, and on and on, leaving the real treasures, the truly meaningful items, alone. She filled the bag, and dumped it out in the hall where the appliances Paul bought still sat. In her pathetic state of sorry-for-herself paralysis, she hadn't bothered to return them.

Perfect.

She set up the new toaster, the new timer, lugged the new microwave to the counter and plugged it in. She ripped open the box of microwave popcorn Paul had bought and tossed a pouch into the oven. Two and a half lazy, hands-free minutes later she brought her bowl of steaming perfect popcorn back into the living room, pulled off the dog-haired couch cover and tossed it into the hallway.

Take that.

Half an hour later, she sighed as Mel Gibson, whose body had conveniently aged fifty years in a matter of hours, flew a conveniently available 1930s plane to his true love, who had woken from her coma after he was frozen and who had even more conveniently been widowed.

Tracy sniffled and gave the reunited couple on the screen a glowing smile. So what if it was all too convenient. She loved happy endings. And this one held a special message for her. Mel's character had survived, triumphed in his new world, yet managed to bring his past into his future. He could still fly the old planes, still count on his old love.

Message received.

Tomorrow she'd go to the store. Buy new versions of everything she'd thrown out. Get that air conditioner for her bedroom, and a bed built for two. Replace the porch screens. Do it all. Then she'd rent that luxury car and go back to the city on Friday, in time for Paul's presentation to 21st Century Produce. Talk to her dad about quitting the business, about finding something else to do. Maybe use her money to help other aspiring farmer researchers live more comfortably while their ideas took shape. Dad might miss her, but he'd be glad she was moving on, as he had.

Because a house couldn't make her happy, because land couldn't make her whole and complete and at peace. Now that she'd found Paul, only one thing could.

Herself.

"WHAT THE HELL do you mean she's sick?" Paul stared at Dave, who'd come to Paul's office to deliver the bad news in person. The presentation to 21st Century was due to start in fifteen minutes and the model he'd hired, a friend of Dave's, had come down with a stomach bug.

Served him right for not going through a professional agency that could offer a replacement. But the woman Dave suggested, a woman trying to get her modelling career started, had been so perfect he'd jumped at her. Petite, dark, very much like Tracy, who was of course the inspiration.

God, he missed her. The week had been an agonizing mix, full of frantic busy preparation and empty unsettling anxiety. Had he gotten his message through or just infuriated her? When the fury died down would she move toward him or seal herself off forever in that antique memory factory?

He brought himself back to the more currently pressing nightmare of stress. "Okay, look, there's nothing we can do short of grabbing someone off the street, which isn't very likely in the next fifteen minutes."

Dave shrugged. "I could *try* that."

"If anyone could pull it off, you could." Paul laughed without humor, pulling his collar away from his sweating skin. Everything was supposed to be perfect; everything *had* been perfect. His big shot, his fabulous campaign. Now he was going to have to go out there and ask the 21st Century Produce crowd to use their imaginations like he was a puppeteer at an amateur kiddy show.

So be it.

"At least we've got the still photos." He adjusted his tie and picked up his presentation notes. "They'll have to do. The concept is intact."

"Another thing, Paul."

He glared at Dave. "No more bad news."

"I think Tracy's here. I caught a glimpse of her out in the hall. Thought you might want to know before you went in."

Paul swallowed. He was pretty sure his heart had stopped, except it suddenly began pounding so hard he swore it was making his lapel jump. She was back. Back from the farm. He'd invented excuses to call her office every day last week and the answer had always been the same. Still away, no news about her return.

"Thanks for telling me."

"Good luck, man." Dave came forward and slapped Paul on the back. "I'll hang around to see how it goes, take you out for a— Hey! I gotta idea." He rushed to the door, turned, and rushed back. "Start the presentation five minutes late, okay?"

Paul shook his head. "Dave, I don't think I can tolerate another one of your ideas."

"No." Dave held up his hands. "This is a good one. I feel responsible for this mess, but I can fix it. You got the dress and stuff here?"

Paul pointed to a dry cleaning bag hanging from a hook on his office door. "Yeah, but it won't fit you."

"Ha...ha...ha." Dave lunged for the bag and rushed out of the room.

Paul sighed. If he wasn't so desperate... But even Dave wouldn't take chances with this presentation. Most likely he just remembered girlfriend number six-thousand-thirty-four had short dark hair.

He went over his notes one more time, tapped the cards on top of his desk to align them. *Inhale. Exhale.* Out of his office, down the hall toward the presentation room where Karen and Jim already waited. And possibly Tracy as well. One look at her eyes and he'd know. One look.

He put his hand on the doorknob, focused his energies, his thoughts, tried unsuccessfully to calm his still-sprinting heart, and went in.

Immediately Tracy's father stood, along with two other managers Paul had been introduced to briefly, and Tracy's secretary Mia, whom he hadn't expected to see. Paul smiled and shook Derek Richards's hand warmly, while sick disappointment threatened to expose his heartiness for the act it was.

Where the hell was Tracy? Had Dave made a mistake?

He greeted the other two managers and Mia and moved to the middle of the room, trying to bolster his sagging enthusiasm for the presentation and for life in general. Why wasn't she here? Was she still at the damn farm? Or just down the hall?

"Welcome. I hate to begin a presentation this important to The Word, Inc. with an apology, but a model I hired to be part of a tableau came down sick and we've been unable to find a replacement."

A few murmurs he assumed were disapproving. Paul gritted his teeth and gestured to a corner of the room covered by a black cloth curtain. At his cue, the lights went down in the room, a soft spotlight hit the corner and the curtain drew back.

The audience applauded wildly. Paul took a step forward, not blinking, his arm still outstretched. On the exact replica of the steps to the Richardses' farm he'd had built, dressed in the sexy black minidress, with red lipstick and nails, about to bite into a perfect ripe tomato, sat Tracy.

She broke her pose to smile shyly up at him. He'd never seen anything so gorgeous in his life. She looked tired, but her eyes were calm, not troubled, not flat, not afraid.

Hope began building up a sweet pressure in his chest.

"Hello." He crossed the space between them and extended his hand for a shake, wanting desperately to kiss her until she was out of breath, but too aware of the room full of eyes on him. "This is certainly a surprise. I'm glad you could make it."

She took his hand and squeezed it hard. "I wouldn't miss it."

He held on a few seconds longer than necessary, room full of eyes be damned, to see if she'd pull away. She didn't, but kept her warm, confident gaze on his. The hope grew sweeter.

He drew back, before contact with her drew his thoughts irrevocably away from the professional arena, or before his pants took on a shape the designer had not intended.

Paul moved back to the middle of the room, power and determination back in spades. He gave a quick nod and another spotlight lit a large photograph of the same set, with the original model sitting on the steps. The background colors had been faded nearly to gray, so the black dress, red tomatoes and her red lipstick and nails stood out vibrantly. "This is the image I want for Tracy's Tomatoes."

A gasp from Tracy, and chuckles from her father and the managers.

Paul held up his hands, grinning. "The innuendo in the name is deliberate. What I'm after is the perfect combination of innocence and sophistication. Old-fashioned family tradition, the father who names a product after his beloved daughter, and modern snappy sensuality."

He took a deep breath and turned his head slightly to direct his remarks to Tracy. "I wanted the woman to embody the same contrasting combination. In the campaign she'll always be the epitome of sexy sophistication, in fabulous clothes and jewelry. But her surroundings will always be humble—a farm, a ballpark, a burger joint. What I want to imply is that she can indulge herself and still feel at home anywhere she goes."

Tracy's smile grew so wide he could see it around the tomato in front of her face. Her eyes over the top were clear and direct. "Yes. She can."

Laughter in the room, and applause. Everyone appreciated the joke. Paul cleared his throat, grateful for the brief wave of audience commentary to cover his slide into emotionalism. He understood the real meaning of her words. That they could make it. That she was willing to try. He suddenly wanted this damn presentation he'd focused his entire life toward over with as soon as humanly possible so he could get her out of here, follow up on the promise in her eyes and talk about forever. Then do wildly sexual things to her for hours.

He continued the presentation, showing the other boards, talking about the media they should target, the possibilities for expansion into television and radio, trying to sound as though there was nowhere else in the world he'd rather be.

He wrapped up his talk, took some questions himself, directed others to Karen and Jim, and finally, finally, ushered the group minus Tracy out of the conference room and out of the offices, ready to growl with impatience.

The second the door swung shut behind them, he

dropped the smile from his face, headed back to the conference room and nearly bumped into Karen and Jim.

"Well, boss." Karen slapped him on the back. "I think that went really—"

"Yeah, it was great." He brushed past her, knocked on the conference room door and went in.

TRACY LINGERED behind after Paul escorted his guests out of the room. She had to put her own clothes back on and she had to make sure Paul had gotten the message.

Several minutes of major making out wouldn't hurt either. Seeing him again had made her want him, physically and emotionally, with an ache that she had a feeling wouldn't quit any time soon.

She stepped out of the black dress and grinned at it. Okay, so the way she'd acknowledged her willingness to change had been a little melodramatic. But when Dave approached her with the plan it seemed too good a chance to pass up. And judging by the pop-eyed, drop-jawed look on Paul's face, she'd made a good decision taking a somewhat playful approach to show him the changes in her.

She pulled on her new suit jacket, bought yesterday on a clothes-buying spree that had left her plenty of styles and moods to choose from. Yes. She had enjoyed herself. Yes, she had felt a little guilty, but also giddy and self-indulgent, and definitely eager for Paul to see her in some of the skimpy underthings.

An impatient rapping came at the door. "Tracy?"

"Come in." She smiled, resisting the urge to weave her fingers together. No reason to feel unsettled, just because her emotions were swirling to the point of total meltdown.

"Hi." She stretched the smile to a grin, took two steps toward him, then ran the rest of the way.

He caught her and whirled her around, then kissed her, drew back to stare at her as if he'd never seen anything quite so miraculous, stroked down the side of her face and kissed her again. "God, I'm glad to see you. I was afraid you weren't ever coming back."

"I had some thinking to do. You won't recognize the farm. I made some changes. I want to make more. You'll see when we go back. If...you'd like to sometime." Her words tumbled over themselves in her eagerness to let him know she was ready to meet him halfway.

"I'd like to. Anytime." He smiled, crinkling the corners of his blue-gray eyes. "How about now?"

"Honest?" She laughed at his eagerness. "Now's good. I think we can get there by—"

Mia burst into the room and reared back guiltily at the sight of them. "Oh, sorry! I came all this way to lend Tracy my red lipstick and polish and I forgot to put them back in my purse."

She spotted the makeup and went over on exaggerated tiptoe. "There they are."

"Hey, Colonel." Dave's head peeked around the door. He saw Paul and Tracy together and gave a thumbs-up. Tracy sighed and took a step back. A party. How nice.

"How did the presentation—" Dave glanced toward Mia and froze.

Mia glanced back at Dave and froze as well.

"...You." The word struggled out of Dave's mouth.

"Oh!" Mia walked closer, gazing up in awe at the gentle giant from her five-foot petite frame. "I've found you."

"I'm hit," Dave whispered. "You're The One."

"It's all right there, in your eyes." Mia put a finger to her own face, then reached up toward his. "Like a part of myself that was missing."

"What's your name? I'm Dave."

"Dave. I'm Mia."

"*Mee-a.*" He dropped to his knees. "It's nice to meet you, Mia, will you marry me?"

"Yes." Her face crumpled into happy tears. "Oh, yes. I'll marry you."

Dave swung her tiny form up into his massive arms and carried her out of the room.

"Tracy?" Mia's voice sounded faintly going down the hall. "I'm taking the rest of the day off...."

Tracy and Paul stood staring after the apparently engaged couple, then turned to stare at each other.

Paul blinked. "Did that just happen?"

Tracy burst out laughing and moved back toward him. "From what I remember of our first meeting on the beach, if we hadn't spent so much time fighting it, that could have been us."

"From what I remember, you're right." Paul put his hands on her waist, drew her close. "I'm done fighting.

No more designer everything. No more luxury for luxury's sake. I promise."

"And I promise no more keeping things forever just to keep things the same. Including me." She bit her lip, tried to smile and got all watery-eyed instead. "I love you."

He kissed her lingeringly, driving up the emotional stakes until she felt she would go mad loving him, mad wanting him.

"I love you, too, Tracy."

"Oh, gosh." She drew back before she started crying and ripping off her clothes. Some things were better left to places other than corporate conference rooms.

"You know what?" She attempted a smile that went wavery and crooked. "I'm starving."

He grinned, a sexy grin of understanding and tousled her curls. "Want to go out for pizza on our way to the farm?"

"Pizza?" She pretended surprise. "Is that really what you want?"

"Sausage or pepperoni?"

"Hmm." She pressed herself against him, unable to be out of contact for long. No question. She'd been hit. He was The One.

"Pizza is okay." She grinned and drew her finger across his lips. "But I kind of have a craving for quail eggs and *Loire Crémant*."

Epilogue

Eight Months Later

"WHAT IS THAT on your finger!" Missy squealed the words out and grabbed Tracy's left hand across their table at Louise's, ravenously examining the large diamond.

Tracy laughed and flushed. "You weren't supposed to notice until Allegra got here and I made my announcement."

"Like we could really miss a boulder that size." Cynthia grinned and hugged Tracy fiercely. "I am *so* thrilled for you, honey. After all that angst at the beginning, you guys deserve a little happily ever after."

"Yeah." Missy plunked her chin down on her hands. "How about spreading it around?"

Cynthia rolled her eyes. "If you actually *spoke* to men instead of just reading about them in the personal ads, you might have a better shot."

Missy blushed. "You'll find yours before me, Cynthia."

"Possibly. But I'm going to bust my buns to be the hardest-working most successful businesswoman in Milwaukee so I can win the Foster Award. Someone else will probably go next. Maybe Allegra. Where is she, by the way?"

"Who knows?" Tracy shrugged, turning her ring around and around on her finger, trying to quell the blissful and probably thoroughly irritating smile on her lips. "Maybe she passed someone whose aura was out of whack and she's straightening it for them."

"Probably." Missy giggled and took another peek at Tracy's ring. "That is *so* beautiful. When's the wedding?

"This summer, at our beach house."

"Not at the farm?"

Tracy smiled. "We'll be renovating the farmhouse this summer. I want to put in office space so I can spend time there running the Foundation."

"Helping other mutant vegetable producers achieve the Great American Dream." Cynthia grinned and lifted her martini in a salute. "A much better use of your talents than pushing avocados."

"It's worked out well." She shook her head, not quite able to take in all the changes that had brought her such happiness. "Everything's worked out well, thanks to the Manhunters. Now we just have to—"

"Oh, gosh, sorry I'm late." Allegra arrived at the table and flung herself into the vacant seat, hair not covered by a wig today, but spiked into short brown points, face flushed, brown eyes snapping behind aqua frames. "You'll never guess what happened to me. You'll never, ever in a million billion years guess what just happened to me. Oh my gosh, I can't believe it. He was...I mean it...he was so...I just looked at him and—"

The three women burst out laughing.

Tracy held up her glass to Allegra; Cynthia and Missy followed suit. "Here's to the adventure of our next Manhunter, Allegra Langton."

* * * * *

Join Allegra, Cynthia and Missy on their own Manhunts in a double Duets by Isabel Sharpe on sale next month!